MY LORD PROTECTOR

The Beresford Adventures
Book 2

Cheryl Bolen

Dearest Reader;

Thank you for your support of a small press. At Dragonblade Publishing, we strive to bring you the highest quality Historical Romance from some of the best authors in the business. Without your support, there is no 'us', so we sincerely hope you adore these stories and find some new favorite authors along the way.

Happy Reading!

CEO, Dragonblade Publishing

Additional Dragonblade books by Author Cheryl Bolen

The Beresford Adventures
Lady Mary's Dangerous Encounter (Book 1)
My Lord Protector (Book 2)
With a Little Help from my Lord (Book 3)

PROLOGUE

THE LONGER HIS parents were gone from this earth, the wiser they became. Henry Beresford, the Sixth Earl of Devere, shook his head when recalling his mother's former lament. *You children will put me in my grave.* Now that he'd become as a parent to his three highly impetuous sisters, he well understood that sentiment. Two down, one to go. He hoped to God Harriett, the last unmarried sister, would not have as difficult a time finding her perfect mate as her older sisters had. He could be free of her none too soon.

Sophia had not wed until she was seven-and-twenty. Maryann had married last year at the age of one-and-twenty. Each had come out at seventeen, but between the two, the highly discriminating sisters had turned down five dozen proposals of marriage.

He would definitely be in his grave if Harriett continued with her aggravating ways. He'd lost count of how many servants had left because of the nontraditional pets she provided sanctuary in their home, and now that she'd come out, her interest in males had all but superseded her devotion to animals.

Like her impetuous sisters, Harriett's unconventional behavior had the potential to irreparably tarnish her reputation. Thank God it was his discreet best friend, Alexander Muir, who had spotted her at Green Park—unchaperoned—with that wastrel Hugh Bly.

From his seated position behind his massive desk, he looked up when the library door swung open and a recalcitrant Harriett stood there, her pale blue eyes sorrowful as she met his stern gaze.

For just a moment, he was distracted by her fair prettiness. It never failed to strike him how odd it was that the two oldest siblings—he and Sophia—were possessed of dark hair and eyes while the two youngest sisters were so incredibly fair. Neither parent had been possessed of the blonde hair or blue eyes like Mary and Harriett. Of course, the fourth earl's hair had once been blond.

His attention returned to Harriett. Why in the devil did she always have to be toting some animal? Today it was that huge fluffy gray cat. If he wasn't mistaken, it was the same cat who'd stealthily absconded with Cook's turbot last week.

"Sit," he said in his most severe tone.

Lashes lowered modestly, she complied. The demmed cat had stayed on her lap, looking for all the world as if he—or was it a she?—was taking a nap.

He hated to be too harsh on his youngest sister. After all, he was just as much to blame as she for her behavioral miscues. Once it was clear that Maryann wasn't returning to England, he should have secured the services of a well-bred woman to ensure Harriett comported herself as an unblemished lady at all times.

"I've already spoken to you about your unpardonable assignation with Bly. Even if he had been a reputable man—which I assure you he is not—it would never be acceptable for a young lady of eighteen to be in the presence of a man without the benefit of a chaperon."

With a defiant tilt of her chin, she glared. "It's not likely anything of an improper nature could have occurred in daylight in the presence of dozens of other people."

She had him there. "It's the illusion of impropriety. A maiden cannot risk her good name. Once lost, it can never be recovered. Do you not want to someday marry a gentleman?"

"More than anything."

"Then you must ensure that you're worthy of a gentleman. To that end, I am going to be engaging the services of a well brought-up woman to serve not only as your companion but also as your mentor in propriety. I should have done so before now since you don't have a mother. God knows, I'm wretched at handling sisters."

Her head softly shook. "You're not wretched. It's your wicked sisters who've put such a burden on you. I am massively sorry."

He could never stay angry at the little minx.

CHAPTER ONE

A DISTANT WHIMPER awakened Charlotte Robinson. Her lids flew open. She'd left her window open to enjoy the balmy sea air on this warm summer night. As dark as it was, she knew morning was still hours away.

It was a wonder she'd heard anything over the roar of the waves crashing to shore at the bottom of the cliffs just beyond the walls of Heathergate.

The alarming sound couldn't have come from Mrs. Wyndham. Her bedchamber was in the east wing. Not once in the year that Charlotte had resided in Heathergate's west wing had she been able to hear any sounds emanating from Mrs. Wyndham's chambers.

Then she heard it once again, only fainter this time.

She bolted up, cocking her heard eastward. No one else was at Heathergate tonight. Mrs. Wyndham had insisted all the servants except Charlotte leave. One of Mrs. Wyndham's mysterious callers was to come tonight.

Charlotte got up, threw on a wrapper, and shoved her feet into satin slippers. Even if Mrs. Wyndham had told her to stay in her chambers, Charlotte was possessed of an unshakable feeling that her employer was in danger.

In order to get to the east wing, she had to descend one of the rambling home's twelve staircases to reach the one that would take her to Mrs. Wyndham's wing. As Charlotte neared the ground floor, heavy footsteps pounded across the stone floors. The home's main timbered door was flung open, and the silhouette of a fleeing man was clearly visible.

Mrs. Wyndham's mysterious caller.

That same sense of dread that had filled Charlotte the night of the fire at Babbley gripped her now as she raced to the staircase that led to her employer's chambers. With each hurried step she climbed, Charlotte's heartbeat raced. *Something's gravely wrong.*

As she neared Mrs. Wyndham's lavishly appointed bedchamber, her conviction that something was wrong increased. She came to the open doorway and paused, knocking. "Mrs. Wyndham, are you all right?"

She had known there would be no answer. She entered the room that was lighted by a candelabra on the bedside table. "Mrs. Wyndham?"

The lack of response encouraged her to continue into the chamber, her gaze fanning from the unused fireplace across the floral carpet to . . . Mrs. Wyndham's body lying grotesquely on the floor at the foot of the bed.

Charlotte yelped.

Then she dropped to the floor next to the lifeless-looking body. She was convinced now that the whimpers that awakened her had come from poor Mrs. Wyndham. As Charlotte's shaking hands felt for a pulse, she knew there would be no more whimpers. Her employer was dead.

It was then, beneath the glow of the candelabra, she saw swollen discoloration on Mrs. Wyndham's neck. She'd been strangled to death.

Which meant that man Charlotte had seen fleeing must have been the murderer.

A chill inched up her spine. Tears gushed. Anger boiled within her. More tragedy. Once again, the carpet had been yanked from beneath her, robbing not only her security but also the affection Mrs. Wyndham had shown her.

How different Betsy Wyndham looked in death. The attractive woman whose dress and toilette bespoke impeccable taste had been transformed into something vastly different. Now, in her skimpy night clothes, her hair in disarray, her mouth twisted into something hideous, she looked harsh and old.

All vestiges of her kindliness had been eradicated by this one final, vile act.

The mysteriousness cloaking Charlotte's employer this past year had been answered in these past few moments. A respectable woman did not entertain men in her night clothes. Which meant Betsy Wyndham was not a respectable woman. Now Charlotte understood the source of Mrs. Wyndham's wealth.

Even though her employer was no longer a young woman, it took no great imagination to understand how beautiful she must have been twenty years earlier. Charlotte had heard about women who fell under the protection of rich patrons. As lovely as Betsy Wyndham would have been, she could have been mistress to a duke, perhaps even a Royal Duke.

Charlotte couldn't bear to look at her for another moment. She got to her feet and began to look around the chamber. That's when she noticed the drawers of Mrs. Wyndham's dressing table gaped open, their contents tossed to the carpet.

Had the murderer stolen her jewels?

Charlotte crossed the pale blue bedchamber to the adjoining study and gasped at what she saw there. Everything that had been on or in the desk had been tossed to the floor, and every book from the white and gilt bookcases had been stripped from the shelves and added to the mountain of haphazardly thrown books that littered the blue carpet.

Charlotte's brows lowered. He wouldn't have been looking for jewels in the study.

It was then that Charlotte remembered something her employee had told her six weeks earlier. "If something should ever happen to me, you're to open this box. Until then, you must hide it in a safe place." She'd given Charlotte a paper-wrapped box the size of a small book.

Charlotte had given her word she would never open the box unless her employer were dead. In the year they had known one another, Betsy Wyndham had come to trust Charlotte completely. She'd told Charlotte she inherently knew their first meeting that truth as well as discretion were guiding principles of Charlotte Robinson's life.

Now was the time for Charlotte to go to her bedchamber and unwrap that box.

She fetched it from the bottom of the worn valise she kept at the bottom of her linen press and took it to the settee in her feminine bedchamber of soft green and cream. First, she untied the knotted string that bound the box, then she tore off the paper and opened the box. It held a small journal as well as a neatly folded letter. On both, she recognized Mrs. Wyndham's messy handwriting.

She unfolded the letter and began to read.

My Dear Charlotte,

If you're reading this, there's a good likelihood my wicked past has caught up with me. I cannot say it was unexpected. It's fitting that an evil person meets an evil end.

My biggest regret is that I may have endangered you. Had I been fortunate to have had a daughter, I wish she could have been you. You're the purest, brightest thing that's entered my life.

You must leave Heathergate immediately. It was no great generosity on my part that you've been so well compensated. I feared you might need funds to flee in the event of my demise. Take all the money you've saved while in my employ and go as far away from Devon as you can. Change your name because I fear there will be those who will want to hunt you down.

I shouldn't give you this journal because having it might endanger you, but it is also more valuable than a king's jewels.

One day you must decide what to do with it. I cannot.

Remember, trust no one.

Tears rolling down her cheeks, Charlotte put both back into the box and stashed them in her valise. She would never believe someone as kindly as Mrs. Wyndham was evil.

She pondered the message for several minutes before making her decision.

Then she began to throw her modest wardrobe into the valise.

She would leave tonight so she could move under the blanket of darkness. She didn't want to end up like poor Mrs. Wyndham.

THERE WAS NO light in Jericho Hutchings' cottage down at the cove. As beastly as she felt about awakening him, Charlotte knew he would welcome the extra money she was prepared to offer him. The past two weeks of fair weather had not brought enough prosperity to these fishermen who'd been battered by ferocious winter and springtime storms. They had only barely been able to eke out a living this year.

It was a few minutes before the old fisherman answered her knock. He would have had to dress himself first. Even when he finally answered the door, he did not at first recognize her in the dark.

"It's Miss Robinson," Charlotte said.

"Has something happened to Mrs. Wyndham?"

Her stomach twisted. She bit her lip. She nodded solemnly. "Someone came to the house and killed her. I... had to escape before he got me." A slight prevarication. It troubled Charlotte to lie. She never lied.

He sputtered out the door of his modest cottage. "Let me at him!"

She put a hand to the old man's wiry arm that was as solid as stone. "No, please. I need to hire your boat. You must take me away from here."

"But what about the murderer? I'll round up the rest of the fishermen, and we can get him!"

She shook her head. "He's gone now, but I fear he'll come back for me. Please. Just take me away. I'll pay you twenty guineas." She doubted he'd earned that much money in the past half-year.

"You're sure he's gone?"

"Yes."

He nodded. "Where are we going?"

She'd not given it any thought. "As far away as you can take me."

It HAD BEEN a week since he'd choked the life from Betsy Wyndham and, finally, he spotted her name in one of the London newspapers, but the headline shocked him.

**Former Courtesan's
Companion Flees
After Killing Her
Generous Mistress**

Betsy had a companion? Why had he never encountered her? That conniving, blackmailing, debauched Cyprian had sworn that she'd sent all her servants away that night. Had the companion, Miss Charlotte Robinson, been there? Could she identify him? Was it possible Betsy had entrusted the girl with her book?

He had to find Charlotte Robinson.

CHAPTER TWO

HER MONEY WAS already running out. Charlotte had given Jericho Hutchings even more than she'd promised once they had hit upon the idea of sailing all the way to the River Thames and ending up in London on a foggy, gray morning. When he'd set her down at the London docks, she'd pressed thirty guineas into his weathered palm.

"I must beg that you tell no one I hired you," she said. "And no one must ever know where you've taken me."

"Aye, miss. I will never betray your trust."

She had eschewed the idea of being set down at a port like Portsmouth where she could have taken the stagecoach on to London because it would have been too risky. Were someone attempting to find her, chances of detection were greater when the number of contacts increased. The much more time-consuming seaside route held more appeal because only one person was entrusted with her itinerary, and she'd known she could count on Jericho's discretion.

The decision to come to London had not been made lightly. Even though it should be easy to adopt anonymity in the world's most populous city, she had worried that she would be recognized. In that earlier life of hers, she had come to the Capital every Season. But this time, it wasn't likely she would be moving in those same prominent social circles.

She'd been forced to spend more of her rapidly dwindling coin on lodgings in Marylebone, a neighborhood she deemed to be relatively safe. She would not begrudge a farthing that went toward something that could help protect her against craven miscreants like the one who'd murdered Mrs. Wyndham.

Even after all these days, she'd been unable to purge from her memory the vision of poor Mrs. Wyndham's distorted corpse.

Now it was imperative that Charlotte find employment, and she believed she would be able to do so with aid from the sister of her old nurse, one Miss Fletcher, proprietress of Miss Fletcher's Domestic Assistance Agency for Discriminating Employers.

The agency that catered to London's elite was located just off Bond Street. Charlotte had worn her best daytime dress, a fairly fashionable muslin sprigged with yellow flowers. Most importantly, it was clean and freshly pressed. She drew in a deep breath and entered the establishment.

Seated behind a feminine desk sat a woman who looked remarkably like Miss Hannah Fletcher, Charlotte's cherished old nurse. Charlotte froze in the doorway. "You look so much like Hannah."

The woman with faded and gray speckled brown hair looked up and studied Charlotte. A smile tweaked at her lips. "And you must be Miss Charlotte Robinson. Please come in."

Charlotte nodded. "I have come to you for help."

The older woman nodded. "Sit down." She indicated an armchair upholstered in crimson velvet. Once Charlotte sat, she said, "I know you didn't do it."

Charlotte's brows lowered. "Do what?"

Miss Fletcher's gaze dropped to the newspaper on her desk. She handed it to her visitor.

As Charlotte read about Mrs. Wyndham's murder, she gasped. "No! This is a lie!" She was horrified that anyone could think she was a murderer. She was especially horrified at the notion of killing a person who had been so kind to her. She had nothing to gain from her former employer's death and everything to lose.

"Tell me what happened," Miss Fletcher encouraged.

"I never knew that Mrs. Wyndham had been a courtesan. I went to work for her a year ago, and . . . I loved her. She was wonderful to me. I would never have hurt her." Charlotte made a conscious decision she would tell no one about the journal. She had never even tried to read it herself. She wanted only to remember Mrs. Wyndham as the kindly woman she'd always been to Charlotte. "After I discovered her body, I found the letter Mrs. Wyndham had given to me to read in the event of her death. In it, she told me I might be in danger and that I needed to leave, to change my name."

Miss Fletcher had nodded throughout Charlotte's tale. "My sister loved you dearly. She said you were possessed of a most tender heart. My sister was a perceptive judge of character."

"Your sister was as a mother to me. No one—not even my Papa—was ever more important in my life."

"I know. I wish she were still alive. She would give her life to help you, and now that she's gone, I will do whatever I can to assist you."

"It will be difficult for one with a new identity and no references to secure employment."

"I can handle that. I hope I don't flatter myself that my firm's reputation is such that any young lady referred by Miss Fletcher's Domestic Assistance Agency for Discriminating Employers is considered beyond reproach." She pursed her lips in thought. "I shall have to determine who will be a good candidate to *recommend* you. It would be best if they have just died . . ."

Charlotte wondered how a dead person could be called upon to write a glowing reference. How could she ever repay this woman for her kindness?

Miss Fletcher's face brightened. "I do have a perfect candidate! Mrs. Smythe-Higgins of Shropshire. No one in London knows anyone in Shropshire. You will have been in service as a companion to Mrs. Smythe-Higgins, recently deceased. Now what shall be your name?"

"I think it will be easier to remember if I retain the same initials."

"A good plan. You must become a Caroline, like the regent's wife. That should be easy to remember."

Charlotte nodded. "It's a fine name. What do you think of Caroline Rutherford?" Her Papa's closest friend at Oxford had borne the surname Rutherford. It had a solid, dependable sound, and by associating it with her father's friend, she ought to be able to remember it.

"It sounds very good to my ears." The older woman drilled her with a stern gaze. "From this point forward, you *are* Caroline Rutherford. Charlotte Robinson has vanished from the face of the earth."

Five-and-twenty years of existence eradicated in one moment. What did it matter? Those she had loved—Papa, her brother, Hannah, and Mrs. Wyndham—were all gone. Her new life was about to begin, though she doubted if she would ever again know what it was to be loved. Or to be happy.

"Now we have to invent your background. My discriminating employers will want to be assured you have been brought up properly. It's best even if you're from a noble family that's become impoverished, though I can't give you a titled forbearer because those things are too easy to verify with *Debrett's* and such."

Her family, though not aristocratic, would have been well known and well respected, but using them was completely out of the question. "We'd best not use anything associated with Parliament."

"Good point." Miss Fletcher got lost in thought once more.

"You are significantly more experienced in these matters than I. You will know what qualities your prospective employers seek."

"Since Mrs. Smythe-Higgins lived in Shropshire, I think your family should also have lived there. Let's say your father was a vicar with a large brood. The fact that he's a clergyman attests to his reverence for education and breeding, and his extensive progeny explains why his daughters would be forced to make their own way in the world."

"But what if I'm asked the name of his parish or village?"

"You must say he moved often. Study a map and learn the name of some Shropshire villages."

Caroline nodded.

"You know, I shall be quite excited," Miss Fletcher said. "I may have already found the perfect position for you. The Earl of Devere was here this morning. He's seeking a well-bred woman to mentor the flighty younger sister for whom he's responsible."

THE WOMAN SENT from Miss Fletcher's was younger than Devere had expected. She was only a few years older than the hoydenish girl she was to guide. His first instinct was to send Miss Rutherford away, but the more he thought about it, the more convinced he became that Harriett might respond more positively to one closer to her own age.

But it was imperative he be convinced of this girl's maturity. How was he to gauge her wisdom in a short meeting like this?

When Miss Caroline Rutherford had gracefully crossed the library floor to take a seat in front of his desk, he'd watched her. In height and build—both average—she resembled Harriett, who was much admired by members of the opposite gender, though this woman was not as pretty as his sister, and her coloring not as striking as Harriett's wide blue eyes and pale, blonde hair. Miss Rutherford dressed respectably in one of those muslin dresses the ladies favored these days.

His first impression that she was plain was soon abandoned. While her warm brown hair and lichen eyes were certainly nothing out of the ordinary, he found her quietly pretty.

That impression was reinforced when she spoke. Her melodic voice was utterly feminine but not in the least like Harriett, whose voice was rarely free of exuberance or hyperbole. Miss Rutherford spoke in measured phrases, appearing to give thought to each word. A vast departure from his sister.

"My sister is just eighteen and needs someone to rein in her impetuousness." He drew a long breath. "I am concerned, Miss Rutherford, that you may be too young. May I ask your age?"

"Of course. I'm five-and-twenty."

"That should be enough age difference. You sound more mature than you look."

A smile transformed her somber face. "Twenty years hence, I should consider it a compliment if one still thinks I look younger than my years."

He chuckled as he looked over the report Miss Fletcher had sent about this candidate. Oddly, this was the sole candidate Miss Fletcher had recommended—and glowingly so, which Miss Fletcher had never before done in all their dealings. Obviously, Miss Fletcher believed Caroline Rutherford was the ideal person for the position, and he had confidence in the woman's judgment. Her recommendations had never disappointed.

"Since your father was a clergyman, I am assured of your principles and education, but I'm not sure your humble origins are sufficient to navigate my sister through London Society. Protocol at country assemblies is vastly different than for balls at Almack's."

She nodded. "But I've been to Almack's, my lord. You see, my father's sister, God rest her soul, saw to it her nieces were presented." Her shoulders shrugged. "I'm afraid I didn't take. It's a challenge to attract a husband when one has no dowry."

It was too true that one without dowry suffered a nearly insurmountable handicap when attempting to attract a husband. Were it not for her absence of dowry, he had no doubts the not-unattractive lady would have met with success on the Marriage Mart. "Then you have been presented at Court?"

"It's a long while ago. I scarcely think of those days now, but yes, I was."

Another of life's inequities. His sister had advantages of prettiness, rank, and a generous dowry. She would no doubt receive many proposals of marriage. What a shame that Miss Rutherford, who was probably possessed of more sense than Harriett, was destined to spend her life as a paid spinster companion.

He leaned back in his chair, fingertips pressed together, as he regarded her. "What kind of advice would you give a girl who was about to go to Almack's or a similar setting?"

She did not hesitate before responding. "A lady should refrain from flirting. Her attentions should not be bestowed exclusively upon any one gentleman. No more than two dances with the same man. She should never attempt to dominate conversations, and she should especially avoid prefacing sentences with the first person. No young lady in my charge would ever be permitted to leave the ballroom with a man. No clandestine meetings in the library or in the garden. The worth of a chaperon is more precious than jewels and should never be dismissed until the young lady is betrothed."

Exactly what he needed to hear. Moreover, the fact she'd answered so readily demonstrated that correct behavior had been ingrained into her. He stood. "It is my privilege to welcome you to the Beresford household, Miss Rutherford." Then, for reasons he could not comprehend, he added. "You will be treated here as a member of our family."

CAROLINE'S BEDCHAMBER AT Devere House was every bit as nice as the one she had so enjoyed at Mrs. Wyndham's Heathergate. Its walls were a sunny yellow, and silken fabrics in the same shade draped her full tester bed. A pair of yellow Sevres vases adorned the marble chimneypiece, and a blue carpet patterned with gold acanthus leaves stretched from wall to wall, making for a warm, comforting chamber.

Though Caroline had nothing of value, she felt compelled to find a secure hiding place for Mrs. Wyndham's journal. She owed it to the woman's memory to protect it from others' eyes.

She looked around the chamber. Though the journal would have fit in the Sevres vases, that was too obvious a hiding place. As were any of the chamber's drawers. Under the mattress was also an obvious place. She couldn't keep it in her valise. What, then?

Her chamber, she finally decided, offered no good options for hiding the journal, but his lordship's library did. His cozy, wood-paneled chamber with its rows and rows of Greek and Latin classics would be little used. She would wait until everyone was sleeping and tiptoe downstairs to find a secure place for the slim volume.

She sat before a gilt dressing table to style her hair. She had never considered herself vain before but, tonight, she wished to look her best. Because of Lord Devere. Even though he'd said she would be treated as a member of the family, she could not believe a handsome aristocrat like him would ever really think of someone like her as a Person Who Mattered. Nevertheless, she could not suppress this unexpected desire to appear attractive whenever she was in his presence.

Not that she would ever expect him to notice. Rest assured, when a man with all his attributes chose a woman, that woman would be in possession of great beauty, rank, and a hefty dowry— all things a mouse like Caroline lacked.

Once she was convinced she had done everything possible to make an agreeable appearance, Caroline got up from her dressing table and stood several feet back to examine herself in its mirror. She wore the only dress she possessed that was suitable for dinner at the home of an earl. Unfortunately, it was the same one she had worn to her interview with the earl that afternoon. Its soft green fabric scooped low at the neckline, and its little puff sleeves dipped barely off her shoulders. Quite a large expanse of skin showed, which always made her feel a bit uncomfortable but which she also knew to be the fashion.

With the generous salary his lordship had agreed to pay her, she would be able to purchase fabric from which she could sew another dress or two so she wouldn't have to wear the same one every night.

The last thing she did before meeting at the family's dinner table was to clasp around her neck a single string of pearls—left to her after the death of the mother she could not remember.

In the dinner room, Lord Devere sat at the head of the table, and a lovely young blonde was seated at his left. His lordship looked up when she entered, and to her amazement, he stood to greet her as enthusiastically as he would have had she been a duchess.

When she had first met him, she'd been so overwhelmed to discover Lord Devere was youngish and handsome, she had not been able to study him as she now could. He was above average in height, and his build was all that was manly and pleasing—so much so that she felt awkward looking him squarely in the eyes. Everything about him was perfection. In spite of his amiability, she felt unworthy to be at the table of this paragon of masculinity.

Because his hair was so dark a brown—like his eyes—she wasn't sure now that the slender blonde beside him could possibly be his sister. The two looked nothing alike.

He then turned to the chamber's other occupant. "Harriett, may I present to you the lady who has done us the goodness to come and be your companion, Miss Caroline Rutherford."

Lady Harriett also stood and returned Caroline's curtsy. "Oh, Devere did not tell me how young and pretty you are."

Caroline rolled her eyes. "You are very kind to imbue me with two qualities I do not possess."

"I believe my sister finds you young compared to the ancient ogre who is her brother."

Caroline bestowed a smile at him before she tucked herself

into the chair he had indicated at his right. "I dare say it must be a Beresford family trait to exaggerate."

"Does that mean you doubt I'm an ogre?" he asked, amusement shining in his dark eyes.

"I am not qualified to answer that question, my lord." Caroline looked across the table to his sister. "What do you think, Lady Harriett?"

The lady giggled. "I confess, I agree with my brother. He can be a beastly ogre."

Now Caroline dipped her spoon into the soup bowl and smiled. The atmosphere at the earl's table was not going to be stiff and oppressive, as she had feared. She only hoped Lady Harriett would prove to be as delightful as she seemed upon this first acquaintance.

That these two held a genuine fondness for each other brought to mind Caroline's closeness to her own brother. Which made her grieve for him afresh.

"Did you find your chamber agreeable, Miss Rutherford?" Lord Devere asked.

"Very much so. I am honored that you've assigned me a chamber on the same floor as the family." She knew enough about the nobility to know that servants—and that's what she was—were not normally accorded such accommodations. It was, indeed, an honor to be treated in such a manner.

"I said you'd be treated as a member of our family." Those brown eyes of his regarded her seriously.

Lady Harriett nodded. "Devere is possessed of a massive reverence for the truth. He never lies."

When the soup was finished, the footman in royal blue livery spooned meat pie onto their plates.

"Do you play cards, Miss Rutherford?" Lord Devere asked.

Her first thought was that it was difficult to find card games at which three could play. "I do."

"Good. You and Harriett can play after dinner. I'll be going to my club."

Caroline was mildly disappointed that he would be leaving but happy to have the opportunity to get to know Lady Harriett better.

"We are quite honored tonight to have my brother dine with us. He often eats at his club."

Caroline believed it neglectful of Lord Devere to leave his orphan sister alone every night, but expressing her opinion would be unwise and unwelcome, especially given his generosity to her. She smiled at Lady Harriett. "I confess I'm looking forward to getting to know you."

"I feel the same. As agreeable as it is to have a live-in companion so close to my own age, I dare say I'm looking even more forward to being able to resume attendance at balls and fetes. The Ogre put his big foot down, prohibiting me from going out into the public until I had a proper chaperon."

Caroline bit her tongue to keep from scolding his lordship for being so overbearing to his sister. Then it occurred to her that the sister must have done something rash that resulted in her brother's stern mandate. "It will be my privilege to accompany you."

"I have decided that unlike my married sisters I shall be wed by the end of this year," Lady Harriett said. "They were both so particular they rejected hundreds of proposals before eventually settling down."

Caroline's brows lowered. "Do you think that a wise course? Would it not be better to marry when one finds the perfect mate? As your sisters must have shown, sometimes it may take a while before one's life's companion enters one's sphere."

"Well put, Miss Rutherford." Lord Devere turned to his sister. "And your sisters did not reject *hundreds* of suitors."

She shrugged. "Seven-and-forty for Sophia and thirteen for Maryann—or Mary as she now calls herself. How many is that?"

"Sixty." He shot an amused gaze to Caroline. "I suppose that is rather a lot."

"What about you, Miss Rutherford?" Lady Harriett asked.

"How many proposals have you turned down? I'm sure a lovely lady like you has broken many a heart."

Lady Harriett hit closer to the mark than Caroline cared to admit. She shrugged. "You see I am still a spinster at five-and-twenty."

"Ah, but you did not answer my sister's question."

Her present life was a lie. She hated to keep piling on more lies. She *had* been like the discriminating Beresford sisters, on a much lesser scale. While her father was alive, she'd been too particular to accept those who proposed marriage. After he died, no one wanted a woman without dowry. "I will own that I may have turned down one or more proposals." Then she cast her attention at the maiden across the table from her. "I was not so eager to be wed as you."

"Do you have regrets?" Lady Harriett asked.

Caroline shook her head adamantly. "Never. I would rather be in service than be shackled to a man I did not love." She turned to the man who had employed her. "Though my feelings may have been different had I not had the good fortune to serve in homes where I've felt useful and valued."

"I hope you will always feel valued here, Miss Rutherford," he said.

CHAPTER THREE

IT MIGHT BE premature, but Caroline felt as if good fortune had twice now smiled on her in the two employers she'd had. Lord Devere was proving to be as good to her as Mrs. Wyndham had been. It helped compensate for the misfortunes of her life.

Even her fears that Lady Harriett would be spoiled, head-strong, and resistant to a stranger's authority proved to be unfounded. The sweet girl had gravitated to Caroline like a needy babe for its mother's affection.

After Devere took his leave that night, the two ladies es-chewed the card table and settled on a sofa in the drawing room. "Will you be terribly disappointed if we don't play cards?" Lady Harriett had asked.

"Not at all. What is it you wish to do?"

Lady Harriett offered her a smile. "I'd like for us to get to know one another better. I'm smashingly thrilled The Ogre selected a pretty young woman to be my . . . new friend."

How kind the girl was not to refer to her as a paid compan-ion. "I don't feel young, and my looking glass tells me I'm no beauty, but I am grateful for your generous description."

"I had feared my brother would saddle me with an octogenar-ian who screwed a *pince-nez* into her eyeball."

Caroline found herself giggling at the image. Even though she knew she was no beauty, she was, nevertheless, grateful that

Lady Harriett found her pretty. "You must tell me what things you enjoy," she said to Lady Harriett.

"Suitors." A liveliness marked the young lady's facial expressions when she began to speak. "I've always dreamed of having a drawing room full of gentleman callers offering nosegays and poorly written poetry. Exactly what my elder sisters experienced." As she spoke, a giant marmalade cat leapt onto her lap. To Caroline's astonishment, Lady Harriett nuzzled her face into the cat's and kissed its small, bow-shaped mouth. "And I adore creatures. All kinds." The lady commenced to lovingly stroke the animal.

"That's a lovely cat you've got there."

"This is Pumpkin. I have two other cats, but don't tell Devere. He would find that excessive. Luckily, he pays so little attention to them, he doesn't remember what any of them look like."

"I don't mean to sound like an ogre, but do you not think it best to be honest with your brother?"

"Oh, I would never lie to him. I just may not always tell the complete truth."

Caroline would not fault the girl for such thinking. She was thankful that Lady Harriett disliked lying. Before the recent calamity that stole her identity, Caroline, too, had abhorred dishonesty. Living a lie was almost as intolerable as losing a loved one. In a way, she had lost someone. Herself.

She must turn her thoughts to a more pleasant topic. "I take it your brother doesn't like cats."

"You are right, though he doesn't admit it. He only likes dogs and horses, and those mostly just at Hamberly. Oh, I am so glad you'll be accompanying me to Hamberly at the end of the Season. Since Maryann married, it's been wretchedly lonely in Yorkshire, especially during those bitterly cold winters."

"I shall be happy to accompany you. Do you like the country?"

"No." The girl wrinkled her nose and shook her head as if

she'd just sucked a lemon. "I thrive in London, and now that you're with me, I'll be able to mingle in Society again. Speaking of which . . . since you're to be attending these fetes with me, Devere has authorized us to go shopping tomorrow. He says you're to be dressed as well as me. I dare say he wants you to appear as a member of the family."

Rather than a woman hired to rein in a wayward sister. Caroline was stunned. Devere had never mentioned that in addition to the generous salary he'd offered, he would be providing her a wardrobe fit for a member of the *ton*. Though she was no slave to fashion, it pleased her that at the balls and routs she would not stand out like a poor cousin. "That's so thoughtful of your brother."

"I suppose it is. It cannot be easy being responsible for an eighteen-year-old sister." Lady Harriett shrugged. "He knows how much I love fashion. I declare, that's another of my passions! You are learning everything there is to know about me, Miss Rutherford. I am greatly looking forward to tomorrow."

"I shall be most grateful to have your advice for I'm woefully derelict in my knowledge of what's fashionable."

"But your dress is testament to the fact you're not ignorant of fashion."

"That's because my last employer selected it for me." Which was true. Mrs. Wyndham had somehow contrived to have a talented dressmaker fashion it for her as a surprise. "And you wouldn't know it, but it's the same dress I wore this afternoon, owing to the fact I own nothing else suitable for dinner at an earl's table. I do know enough about fashion to know that I committed a *faux pas* by not dressing for dinner."

"You mustn't worry you'll commit any more *faux pas*. It will be my absolute pleasure to take you under my wing, so to speak. We'll have such a great time selecting your wardrobe."

Wardrobe? That sounded exceedingly expensive. Lord Devere must be very rich. And she was very beholden. "Will you be getting new finery also?" Caroline asked.

The young woman shook her head. "No. I previously acquired a wardrobe for the Season." She shrugged. "It's just that my Season was cut short. I've had to wait to resume it until you arrived."

Was Lady Harriett going to tell her of the transgression that brought her Season to a halt? It wasn't Caroline's place to pry. "Then I dare say you're as happy that I've come as I am happy to be here."

Lady Harriett nodded. "Did my brother tell you what I did that so angered him?"

"No."

"Then I may as well. I assure you, it was perfectly innocent."

Caroline's eyebrows elevated.

"I went by myself to Green Park where I met a man my brother considered highly ineligible."

"I appreciate your honesty and hope you'll always feel free to confide in me, although I cannot promise not to be didactic. I owe it to you and to your brother to ensure that your behavior remains above reproach. Now, to put on my chiding cap, I must tell you that even if the young man you met in Green Park had been above reproach, you should not have met *any* man without a chaperon."

"I know. It's all about how things look."

"Indeed it is. I cannot stress too much how important it is to your future happiness that it not be tarnished now by rash decisions."

"You will be good for me, Miss Rutherford."

"I will always have your best interest at heart."

LONG AFTER LADY Harriett had retired to her chambers for the night, and Caroline had brushed her hair, washed her face, and donned her night shift, Caroline slipped on a wrapper and grabbed Mrs. Wyndham's journal and a candelabra.

She quietly left her room and padded softly along the corridor. When she came to the top of the stairs, she realized all the candles had been extinguished, save for one sconce casting a buttery glow on most of the staircase.

As quietly as she could, she descended the stairs. When she reached the ground floor, where his lordship's library was located, she paused and made sure no one was there. Then she advanced to the library, glad she'd brought her own illumination into the room's inky darkness.

She surveyed the rows of books, and then went to the seemingly little-used Latin classics. Just behind the faded red leather books on the next-to-highest shelf, she dropped Mrs. Wyndham's book. She prayed this book is not what caused her former mistress' death.

A door closed, and heavy footsteps came near. Could it be Lord Devere? If it was, and if he were coming here, she had best pretend she was looking for a book to read.

She moved away from the Latin titles just as the door opened. Her heart pounding prodigiously, she looked into the piercing gaze of Lord Devere. He was fully dressed in evening clothes. She had not accounted for the likelihood he would be coming home from his club.

His dark eyes whisked over her dress. Or her state of undress.

"I do hope it's permissible to select a book from your library?" she said, not without a tremble in her voice.

"Of course."

"I . . . couldn't sleep. I apologize for not asking your permission."

"No need. I said for you to feel like a member of the family. Perhaps I can help you find something to read."

"Rousseau?"

His brows raised. "Then you're enlightened?"

She offered a weak smile. She was still gripped by nervousness. "I aspire to be so."

He went to a shoulder-high shelf behind her and retrieved a thick book of rich green leather and presented it to her. "I'm indebted to you for bringing the candles. I was coming to fetch a book myself."

He went to another shelf and withdrew a book. She glimpsed the title *Rights of Man*.

"You are truly enlightened," she said to him, this time freely offering a smile.

He took the candelabra from her hands. "It's my duty to escort the lady back to her chamber. Besides, mine is just beyond yours."

How fortunate she was to have come to Devere House. She'd never heard of an employee being treated as one of the family and having quarters right next to them.

Had she known she would see his lordship, she would not have brushed out her hair or washed the rouge from her cheeks. She could only pray the candlelight was so dim he'd not been able to notice how dowdy she looked.

Not that it mattered to anyone except her. His lordship certainly would not be paying attention to most common-looking commoner.

They climbed the stairs in silence, and when they reached her chamber door, he returned her candelabra. "Good night, Miss Rutherford. I hope you enjoy Rousseau. And I hope he puts you to sleep."

How could she go to sleep when her nerves had been stretched so tautly? Her breathing had yet to be restored to normal.

"OH, MISS RUTHERFORD! You will be the prettiest lady in the *ton* in that fetching gown."

Thus far, they had spent over three hours at Madame

Blanche's establishment on Bond Street and had—with Lady Harriett's discerning eye—selected three morning dresses (one with a matching pelisse), three evening dresses, and now were in the process of selecting the third ball gown for Caroline.

They had pored over the pattern books and had looked at over a hundred materials of varying colors and fabric ranging from sheer muslin to plush velvet. Without Lady Harriett, Caroline would have floundered. She had been so long away from Society that she was clueless about what would now be deemed stylish.

Caroline lacked Lady Harriett's talent for envisioning. How could one tell anything from a length of lavender fabric draped over Caroline's shoulder?

Never in her five-and-twenty years had Miss Caroline Rutherford—or her former Charlotte Robinson—ever been indulged in so spendthrift a manner. She would be lying if she said she wasn't enjoying every minute of it. Truth to tell, since adulthood, she had possessed only one dress that had not been stitched by her own hand.

She would have been exceedingly grateful if Lord Devere had provided her with a few bolts of fabric from which to sew her new finery. Being indulged as she had been today did not happen to plain women in service at the homes of the nobility. What a wonderful employer Lord Devere was.

Madame Blanche herself had given all her attention to Caroline, even though other customers were in her shop. Did the modiste believe Caroline was actually a member of the Earl of Devere's family? Once all the selections were made, the modiste agreed to start sending the dresses to Devere House on Curzon Street as each was completed. "I shall have seamstresses working around the clock."

"Oh, that's not necessary," Caroline protested.

Mrs. Blanche, who spoke in heavily accented French, shook her head. "It is something upon which I insist. It's a great honor to have the patronage of Lord Devere . . ." She looked at Lady

Harriett. "And his delightful sister. Nothing less than their total satisfaction—and yours too, Miss Rutherford—will do."

Caroline was pleasantly surprised that upon leaving Madame Blanche's establishment, Harriett said she was taking her to her favorite glove shop and milliner's on nearby Conduit Street. She would have protested had it not been for her desire to please Lady Harriett and her brother.

"You will have your first gown in time for tomorrow night's ball at Lady Atherton's," Lady Harriett said.

"Surely not that fast!"

Lady Harriett's step slowed, and she tossed a mischievous look at her companion. "Madame Blanche meant what she said about being honored by Devere's patronage. I am not supposed to know this, but my brother has spent considerable funds at Madame Blanche's." She lowered her voice. "He lavished his former mistress, the actress Sally Glen, with a wardrobe fit for a queen. It made Madame Blanche the most sought-after modiste in all of London."

So his lordship had a former mistress. Sally Glen. Caroline had once seen her on the stage and thought the raven-haired actress the most beautiful woman she had ever seen. Lord Devere was possessed of a discerning eye.

She found herself wondering if the actress had been replaced. Or had his lordship dismissed her because he'd found a woman he wished to make his countess? Such a woman would be profoundly fortunate.

With urging from Lady Harriett, Caroline acquired four pair of gloves, and across the street from the glove maker's, she ordered one pair of new shoes for day and a pair of satin slippers for night.

By the time they left the shoemaker's, both ladies were so exhausted they were grateful the Devere coach awaited to carry them back to Curzon Street. The youthful tiger who perched on the back of the coach was of great service in handling their packages.

"Thank you, Billy," Lady Harriett said to the lad.

The ladies then settled back into the squabs, and Caroline sighed. "I am embarrassed that I've come to you so ill prepared to mingle in Society."

"Devere assures me you are suited for Society. It's your clothes that are not."

"Your brother is very kind."

"He is. Even if he is an ogre."

Had they been walking, the route to Curzon Street would have been shorter. Traffic snarled on busy Oxford Street. Saddle horses wove in and out among the fine carriages that stalled along the busy street, their drivers shaking their fists at the lone riders on horseback. It took them nearly half an hour to return to Devere House.

"You must come to my chamber," Lady Harriett said.

"And why must I?" Caroline teased.

"Because I want you to select a dress to wear to dinner to-night. I would wager we are the same size."

"I would advise a maiden not to wager," Caroline said with a wink.

"I shall wait until I marry to begin high-stakes wagering."

"Then I dare say you'll need to marry a rich man." Of course, Lady Harriett would no doubt enter marriage with a generous dowry.

As lovely as Caroline's chamber was, Lady Harriett's was even lovelier—and much larger. Her apartments fronted the building, which afforded her a pair of towering casements draped in emerald silk, the same silk that enclosed her large tester bed.

Adjacent to her bedchamber was a dressing room adorned in the same emerald and another marble fireplace, and beyond that chamber was a small study centered by a French escritoire in white and gilt. The emerald and white color scheme carried throughout the three chambers.

They stayed in the dressing chamber as Lady Harriett's maid brought down a variety of gowns. Feeling like the poor cousin did not begin to describe Caroline's amazement over her charge's wardrobe. It seemed incomprehensible that a maiden of eighteen could possibly possess so many dresses—and every one of them remarkably lovely.

"I dare say I would be honored to wear your oldest, least fashionable dress, and I'd feel like a royal princess in it," Caroline said. "They're all so lovely."

The younger lady stood back and shifted her gaze from the half a dozen gowns hanging on hooks around the chamber to the plainly dressed woman beside her. "I think the mint green will do nicely. You must play up your green eyes." She shrugged. "Green doesn't really suit me."

"But blue will most certainly suit you and complement your eyes." Lady Harriett's eyes were a deep indigo.

Caroline tried on the dress, and it fit almost perfectly. She thought perhaps she filled out the bodice a bit fuller than Lady Harriett would have. Was too much of her *décolletage* showing? She felt self-conscious, but realized that exposing one's flesh was perfectly acceptable in the circles in which Lady Harriett traveled. The necklines of all that lady's dresses scooped low. Embarrassingly so, in Caroline's opinion, but she did not want her provincial ways to cause consternation to her employers. She must make every effort to fit in.

She stood back to survey herself in the looking glass, mesmerized over her own appearance. She no longer looked like the dowdy Miss Rutherford. This beautiful gown transformed her into something elegant. And Lady Harriett had been right. The green was most becoming. Never in her five-and-twenty years had Caroline ever appeared to be anything out of the ordinary. Until she donned this dress.

As she stood there, movement in the corner of the chamber caught her eye. She turned to look just as a fat brown mouse came charging at her. She screamed, a shrill elongated note, and leapt up on the tufted silken chair that was closest to her, her heartbeat thumping.

How could something that small so terrify her? She must look a total ninny, standing there on top of the chair, feet above the scurrying mouse that was no bigger than her fist.

Now Lady Harriett was on her knees crawling after the creature, which she managed to squeeze her hand around. Then, to Caroline's astonishment, Lady Harriett began to speak to the offensive mouse in the sweetest tones imaginable. "There, there, Mr. Mousie, did that big lady frighten you?" She petted the soft pelt as she looked up at Caroline. "Pray, Miss Rutherford, don't be afraid of Mr. Mousie. He's a member of our family."

Just then, the door to Lady Harriett's adjacent bedchamber banged open, and Devere came charging into the dressing room. "What's happened? I heard a scream."

CHAPTER FOUR

DEVERE SHOULD, BY now, be accustomed to screaming employees who'd encountered one of Harriett's unorthodox pets. He'd lost the services of many qualified women who could not tolerate coexisting with his sister's live menagerie.

Earlier this year, he'd put his foot down and banned her pet snake from Devere House. The only way he'd won that victory was by sending one of their grooms all the way to Yorkshire to install her bloody snake at Hamberly. Her pets were treated more favorably than half the urchins in the Capital.

He hadn't expected to find the level-headed, demure Miss Rutherford shrieking and looking terror-stricken atop a chair in his sister's dressing room. He quickly deduced the source of her distress. That damned Mr. Mousie. How his sister determined the sex of such a creature, he did not want to know.

He also hadn't expected the woman he'd thought to be quietly pretty to look so alluring. This woman standing on the chair could arouse a marble statue. How had he not previously noticed Miss Rutherford's plump breasts? Or the perfection of her milk-white skin? Had her eyes always been that same shade of pale green?

It was as if an artist had painted this dressing room in ivory and emerald as a setting for this spectacular woman. He fairly lost his breath as his gaze lingered over every inch of her.

There was also a marked vulnerability about her that radically contrasted with the calm maturity and deliberate decision making she'd previously exhibited. That was not to say those characteristics that demonstrated her capabilities were not genuine. He had no doubt of her qualifications to be the steadying influence Harriett needed. He just hadn't expected to see a crack in the lady's ever-confident demeanor.

In spite of the strong exterior she projected, beneath it she was a fragile female.

Perhaps it was that very vulnerability—even more than her lovely appearance—that had blindsided him when he'd walked into this dressing room. She affected him in the same way a stray kitten affected Harriett. He wanted to draw her into his arms and keep her safe.

He strode to the chair that provided her asylum from the fearsome mouse and whipped her into his arms, then quickly restored her to floor. "Forgive me, my dear Miss Rutherford, for not warning you about my sister's creatures."

"It's I who should ask forgiveness for my unpardonable silliness. I am mortified by my own actions."

He'd actually found her fright to be refreshingly charming. "It was not silliness. Lamentably, I know from vast personal experience that most females react to mice in the same manner as you."

Harriett, still plopped on the carpet, nodded. "And to snakes, too."

Miss Rutherford's eyes widened. "Please tell me I will not encounter snakes for I am terrified of them."

Harriett pressed her lips to that damned mouse's fur, then glared at her brother. "Only at Hamberly. Devere won't let me keep them in London anymore."

He addressed Miss Rutherford. "Be assured that when we return to Hamberly, my sister's pet snake will not be permitted indoors."

"That is gratifying."

He shook his head. "How she manages to keep that mouse with all these blasted cats I will never understand."

"It is because I usually keep Mr. Mousie in his own little house where my kitties cannot get to him."

Devere's amused gaze met Miss Rutherford's. "She means cage."

"It's not either a cage. I've fixed his house up with little mouse furnishings." Harriett's gaze returned to her pet mouse. "I'm so sorry, Mr. Mousie, I forgot to lock you in this morning. Those big kitties must have terrified you."

A pity they'd not had him for breakfast. Devere rolled his eyes and spoke to Miss Rutherford. "I most sincerely hope you don't change your mind about staying with us after this encounter."

"I will not." Levity lightening her voice, she playfully added, "At least not before my new dresses are delivered"

He chuckled.

"I've been met with great kindness and generosity here."

Harriett sprang to her feet, still holding that diminutive creature. "Oh, Devere, you should have seen Miss Rutherford at Madame Blanche's! Everything looked so lovely on her. I could tell Madame Blanche was thrilled at the notion of Miss Rutherford displaying her gowns."

Once more, his eyes raked over the lady being discussed. "She does look lovely."

A rose hue climbed into Miss Rutherford's cheeks. The lady was blushing! "This is not one of the new dresses. Your sister was kind enough to loan me one of hers until the first from Madame Blanche's arrives." Her lashes lowered. "I'm very grateful for your generosity."

He brushed off her thanks. "It doesn't signify." Then he offered her his crooked arm. "If my lady is ready for dinner, it will be my pleasure to escort you."

Her blush deepened as he led her to the dinner room on the floor below.

During the first course, she said not a word. Was she practicing what she had preached to Harriett about a lady not dominating the conversation?

"Did you know Miss Rutherford was keen to read your hoard of newspapers this morning, Devere?" his sister asked.

"All of them?" he asked, incredulous, his gaze sweeping to the woman being discussed. Not many men in the Capital subscribed to every one, as he did. He'd never heard of a woman interested in news that mostly centered on Parliamentary occurrences. His sisters, who preferred to pore over the pages of *Ackermann's*, certainly had no interest in matters of government.

Miss Rutherford nodded shyly.

"Are you interested in Parliamentary activities?" he asked.

"I am."

His interest spiked. "May I inquire what you could possibly find interesting?"

The lady shrugged. "All of it, actually, though I'm particularly interested to see if those in the House of Commons will respond to demands for the unification of laborers. And, of course, I applaud the recent efforts against slavery, which I saw that you endorsed, my lord."

That bill had passed last week, before he'd ever contemplated hiring Harriett a companion. That must mean even before she knew she would be living under his roof she still had an interest in bills in which he, too, was interested. How singular. He could not deny he was impressed. He was also impressed that this woman of few words suddenly abandoned her muteness when asked about Parliament. "How do *you* stand on labor unions, Miss Rutherford?"

Her rosy lips pursed. She was quite fetching in an understated but wildly appealing way. "With most peers I would not wish to state my opinion for I fear it would be in opposition to theirs."

"But with me?" He regarded her with amusement.

"I believe I've seen enough of your voting record and your speeches in the House of Lords to gauge your views, my lord."

He set down his wine glass. "Have you now?"

She nodded, the expression on her face reminding him of Harriett when she confessed to adopting another mongrel dog.

"And are you in agreement with those views?" he asked.

"I am, my lord."

"You are referring to labor unions?"

"Yes."

This lady's monosyllabic answers certainly practiced what she preached. "Would you have knowledge of any other possibly controversial programs which I favor?"

"I do."

She was going to force him to drag every syllable from her sweet little mouth. "And what might one be?"

"Rotten boroughs?"

"You're remarkably well informed. How is it you are interested in such matters?"

"My father was."

"The clergyman?"

There was a brief pause before she answered. "Yes."

"I take it he was not a Tory."

"That's correct."

What would it take to loosen her tongue? "So he must have been interested in reform, and I'm guessing you, too, favor more progressive ideas. Would I be correct?"

"You would be, my lord."

"My brother, I am told, is exceedingly progressive," Harriett said.

"At times, I fear he rather shoots himself—or should I say shoots your class?—in the foot." Miss Rutherford was more at ease in addressing his sister.

Harriett raised a quizzing brow. "How is that?"

"Some of the programs he's promulgated—like labor unions—would likely diminish his own fortune in favor of boosting the fortunes of the masses."

"Oh, but Devere has more money than he needs," Harriett

said. "Why should he not contribute to the betterment of the lower classes?"

"You have every right to be proud of your brother's Parliamentary accomplishments."

"I will own, I don't keep up with such matters as I should, but I applaud my brother's efforts."

"That's enough about me." He eyed his sister. "I understand there's a ball tomorrow night."

"Yes, at the Athertons'."

"I plan to accompany you," he said.

Harriett's mouth dropped open as her gaze bounced to Miss Rutherford. "My brother never attends balls."

"I WILL BE the envy of every man at the Athertons' tonight," Devere said as he peered across the carriage at his sister and Miss Rutherford. He spoke the truth. All of his sisters had been acknowledged beauties, and Harriett was no exception. No one would believe Miss Rutherford was not a member of the Beresford family. She wore clothes in the same elegant manner in which she always comported herself, with the exception of leaping upon chairs to avoid mice, he thought, smiling at the memory.

"Do you not adore this creation Madame Blanche designed for Miss Rutherford?" Harriett asked.

He did not pretend to be knowledgeable about women's fashions, but he thought the dress remarkably pretty. The body of her dress was salmon colored with an overdress of ivory lace, the same fabric which formed the little capped sleeves that fell slightly off her pale shoulders. The low-cut bodice, too, was constructed of more of the same ivory lace, bordered with silver cording.

But it wasn't the bodice that drew his attention as much as

what lay within it. How could one as coolly poised as she ignite such a ravenous heat strumming through his veins? Though she was every inch a lady, he could not dispel the notion of removing that dress deliberately and slowly and drawing her close until their bodies melded into one.

In the past, he'd always been drawn to women of extremes, those with either dark exotic looks or to fair women with whitish-blonde hair and limpid blue eyes. Miss Rutherford fell squarely in the middle—dare he say average?—with undistinguished brown hair and lichen eyes, both of which could be found on a majority of young British women. Yet for reasons he could not pinpoint, there was nothing ordinary about Miss Caroline Rutherford.

With or without a dowry, this lovely woman would have no difficulty attracting a bevy of devoted suitors. Unaccountably, the notion of her being courted annoyed him.

He'd been unable to remove his gaze from her during the coach ride from Curzon Street to the Atherton mansion on Piccadilly. "Miss Rutherford does look lovely. No one could be a better advertisement for Madame Blanche."

It was too dark to see her reaction to his comments, but he would wager he'd caused her to blush.

At the ball, he found himself enjoying it more than he'd antic-ipated. He normally avoided balls, but he had to own that watching his sister being greatly admired brought him satisfac-tion. He also enjoyed displaying a possessiveness with Miss Rutherford. It just would not do for her to be such a success that she'd be the recipient of marriage proposals that would take her away from Devere House. The Beresfords needed her. They were good to her and did not want to lose her.

He claimed her for the first set, pleasantly surprised that she remembered the steps since, by her own admission, she had not danced in years. Her behavior—with its absence of flirting and chattiness—exemplified exactly what she was imparting to Harriett and exactly what Harriett needed.

As much as he loved his middle sister, Maryann, he knew

Miss Rutherford was a far better influence on the impressionable Harriett than the impetuous Maryann would have been. Thank God, Maryann had married the fine man who was just what she needed to rein in her flighty personality.

No sooner had the dance commenced than his closest friend, Alex Muir, begged an introduction to his female companion.

"Mr. Muir!" Miss Rutherford greeted. "I am a great admirer of yours."

Though Alex was caught off guard by her comment, Devere immediately knew she was referring to his friend's work in the House of Commons. "Don't get your hopes up, old fellow. Miss Rutherford refers to your efforts in Parliament."

Now Alex's brows hiked. "Is that so?"

"Indeed," she said.

"Miss Rutherford's remarkably well informed on matters of government," Devere explained.

"Oh, I don't know about that," she protested.

"I do," interjected Harriett, who'd rejoined their group after dancing with a young viscount.

Alex directed his attention once more to Miss Rutherford. "I thank you, Miss Rutherford."

"I read the full text of your speech on universal education two weeks ago. It was brilliant," she said. "How I wish I could have been there in person to hear you deliver it."

It seemed as if her comments had increased Alex's height by a foot. He oozed with a confidence he rarely exhibited in the presence of women. "If you would permit me to call upon you, I will recite from memory," he said with a chuckle.

"He's not joking," Devere said. "My friend boasts a perfect memory. He never has to consult notes when delivering a speech."

"And some of his speeches are over an hour in duration," Miss Rutherford added. "I am most impressed."

"I was not joking about wishing to call upon you, Miss Rutherford."

Her shyness returned. "As honored as I would be, I am not in a position to receive callers. I have duties to perform."

Alex looked puzzled.

Devere wasn't about to initiate in this setting an explanation about her duties. He'd meant it when he said she would be treated as a member of his family. He had no intentions of disclosing the nature of her employment at so public a function. In private, he would enlighten his closest friend. "You must feel free to entertain callers," Devere said to her.

"Indeed you should," Harriett encouraged.

Miss Rutherford did not respond.

"I say, old fellow," Devere said, "why don't you come by Curzon Street tomorrow? You'll be able to see Miss Rutherford." That's when he would explain why the lady resided with them.

As close as the two men were, Devere would prefer that his friend not further his acquaintance with Miss Rutherford. She was like the canto of a cherished poem he retrieved in private for his own enjoyment.

"Perhaps the lady will do me the goodness of standing up with me for the next set?" Alex inquired, eyeing the woman in question.

"I should be delighted to."

While they danced, Devere was powerless to keep from watching them. How well suited the two were. They could actually have passed for brother and sister as both were possessed of warm brown hair, green eyes, and average height for their respective genders. Moreover, the two would be intellectually compatible.

Alex preferred talking of government matters more than anything, and it seemed the lady was of the same ilk.

It was only then Devere realized he, too, shared those same qualities. He took his duties in the House of Lords as seriously as he undertook responsibility for his sisters. Perhaps that's why he'd developed this connection to Miss Rutherford. He, too, had much in common with her.

Though he'd thought it would be a nice gesture to stand up with his sister for one dance, the opportunity did not become available. Many young gentlemen in attendance vied with one another for the privilege of dancing with her. Devere had to own she looked most handsome in her pale-yellow gown. And even though she'd only been under Miss Rutherford's influence for two days, he thought he detected a change in his sister. She was less chatty and had about her an air of elegance.

Just like Miss Rutherford. He was very pleased with himself for insisting Harriett have a companion and even more satisfied with his selection.

The last dance of the evening he claimed Miss Rutherford. "If you're not too tired from dancing every set, I should be honored to stand up with you."

"It will be my honor, my lord." She set her white-gloved hand on his proffered sleeve.

"No blisters?" he asked. "You've been a popular lady tonight."

"No blisters."

He wondered if he would ever manage to engage her in a conversation that increased from syllables to complete paragraphs. The country dance afforded no opportunity for further conversation.

In the carriage ride home, he was filled with pride over the appearance and deportment of the two women he'd brought. "You ladies were certainly popular tonight."

"I enjoyed it excessively," Harriett said. "I had no less than five men beg to call on me tomorrow." She turned to Miss Rutherford. "You were a great success, too."

The other lady shrugged. "Your success is all that matters. Your brother must be very proud with how much you were admired."

"I am," he said, "but I'm not such an ogre that I would deprive you, Miss Rutherford, of making conquests of you own."

She immediately shook her head. "The only conquest that matters is Lady Harriett's. She wants to end the Season as a lady betrothed to a worthy man, so that's what I most desire."

But then both ladies would leave Devere House. He didn't like to think of that. Nor did he like to think that his best friend would be calling on Miss Rutherford the next day.

CHAPTER FIVE

SLEEP ELUDED CAROLINE that night. The evening had exhilarated her so much that she felt like a wind-up toy that could not shut down. Lady Harriett had been right. Caroline had been a success, but not necessarily in the way that lady gauged. It mattered not to Caroline that Alexander Muir—a man she greatly admired—was going to call upon her. It mattered not that she had stood up for every set. What mattered was that Lord Devere had danced with her at the beginning of the night and at the end of the night.

And he danced with no other lady.

She cautioned herself not to read too much into his interest in her. He was merely being considerate, trying to ensure that she fit in. After all, his sister's future was linked to her, and his sister was very dear to him. His consideration of Caroline's feelings differed vastly from attraction. His lordship could not be attracted to a woman like she who lacked everything, most especially pedigree. She pictured the beautiful actress Sally Glen. Only women possessed of extraordinary beauty like that could possibly appeal to his lordship. Certainly not a woman as plain as Caroline Rutherford.

During the restless night, she even thought of steeling herself against his potential seduction. She'd heard of employers who took advantage of female servants. Yet even though she had not known Lord Devere for long, she believed him to be an honorable man.

Besides, he had no need to ever seduce an underling like her when every beauty in the *ton* would willingly give herself to so handsome a peer.

Throughout the night, as well as now, she felt like a princess of the blood. No hoard of gold could have meant more to her than Lord Devere's attentions.

She turned from side to side in her cozy feather bed. She added an additional pillow. She coaxed herself to dismiss the memory of dancing with Lord Devere. To no avail.

She could not dismiss the memory of the way he'd gazed at her with such open admiration the previous day in his sister's dressing room. She could not dismiss the memory of him scooping her into his arms when he set her down from that chair. For as long as she lived, she would remember how womanly she'd felt when his lazy gaze lingered over every inch of her. She would recall how honored she felt when he offered his arm to escort her to the dinner room.

Even in those days when she had summoned a good bit of attention from gentlemen in London, her head had never been turned. She had certainly not lost sleep like she was doing tonight. None of those admirers had ever mattered.

Lord Devere mattered.

And she cursed herself for being so foolish.

IT WAS MIDAFTERNOON when Alex entered Devere's library. Devere looked up from his desk where he'd been penning a letter to Miss Fletcher to thank her for sending them Miss Rutherford. This was the first time he had ever written to the lady in praise of one of her selections, though her selections had always been most satisfactory. He set down his pen. "Can I offer you Madeira?"

His friend nodded, then plopped on the sofa. "Pray, tell me

why Miss Rutherford is residing at your home," he said as Devere handed him a glass and came to sit on the opposite end of the sofa.

"After you witnessed Harriett meeting Bly at Green Park, I realized my sister needed a steadying influence."

"Is she a cousin I've never met?"

"No. She was recommended by Miss Fletcher."

Alex's eyes widened. "You don't mean to tell me Miss Rutherford's a paid companion!"

Somehow, hearing Miss Rutherford referred to in such a way sounded offensive. Though she hadn't been long under his roof, Devere had come to think of her as . . . sort of as a member of the family. But altogether different. Still, lumping her in with other employees like his housekeeper was a disservice to Miss Rutherford—not that his housekeeper was not highly valued. He glared at his friend. "I beg that you not refer to Miss Rutherford in such a manner. Even though she's not been long with us, we like to think of her as a member of the family."

Alex's brows hiked. "Like a poor cousin?"

"I suppose so." Though Devere disliked that description also.

"Would that the Muir family had such cousins. The woman's a rare find, to be sure."

"Harriett's delighted with her."

Alex looked askance at him. "What about you, old fellow?"

Devere shrugged. "I am satisfied."

"She not only enlivens conversation your dinner table, but she's also pleasant to peer at."

Devere refused to confess he'd abandoned dining at his club in favor of joining Harriett and Miss Rutherford each night for dinner. "The lady is shy. She doesn't speak a great deal."

Alex chuckled. "I had no problem speaking with her last night. I found her to be remarkably well informed. Quite intelligent, too. Perhaps she's intimidated by your title."

Why was it the ladies in his house found him to be an ogre? He considered himself amiable. "Another handicap to being the son and heir. You'll find out one day." That day couldn't be far away, given his father's advanced age and poor health. His friend was also a first son and would carry his father's title.

"Dare I hope to be as sought after by the ladies as you've been all these years?"

"Be careful what you wish for, old fellow. Being the object of attentions from mothers of plain marriageable daughters is nothing to be coveted."

"You'll get no sympathy from me." Alex took a final swig of his drink and stood. "Now, my dear friend, I shall call on your Miss Rutherford, with your permission, of course."

"You have it," Devere said without enthusiasm. He kept wondering if Miss Rutherford thought him an ogre. Is that why she refused to speak to him in sentences?

BEFORE SHE AND Lady Harriett had entered the drawing room to greet the lady's suitors—three young men had already sent up their cards—Caroline had felt compelled to establish a sign she could make if Lady Harriett were about to commit a breach of decorum. If the lady was chatting excessively or using an unladylike term, Caroline would wipe her brow. Given that it was a summer day, it was a perfectly innocuous gesture to signal the younger lady.

"I don't mean to be ogre-like," Caroline had said, "but I would be derelict in my duties if I ignored any *faux pas* you might commit—not that I anticipate you committing one. Still, we want the same thing from this Season: we want you to attract the perfect husband."

The two ladies sat on the same mint green sofa while Lady Harriett's suitors sat on side chairs that formed a semicircle facing the ladies. Caroline was struck that her ladyship's aspirations were already being met. Each of the men had presented nosegays and slips of poetry written in praise of her beauty.

None of the men would have appealed to Caroline on any level, but she had to own they were all younger than her, and she had never been attracted to young men. Which made her wonder how old Devere was. She would guess him to be at least a half dozen years her senior.

While she was pondering this, Hopkins announced Alexander Muir. She was well aware that the newcomer only had eyes for her as he entered the sunny chamber. His appearance of average height and build, finely tailored clothing, and his stylish medium brown hair were agreeable, though he could not measure up to his friend, the Earl of Devere.

She could tell by the way Bennett Stone gushed over him that Mr. Stone must be an inaugural member of the House of Commons, where Alexander Muir was a powerful voice. "Though my family's always been Tory through and through," the young blond man said, "I would be remiss if I did not use this fortuitous opportunity to praise your recent speech on children's education. It was *almost* enough to make me switch my affiliation."

Mr. Muir shook the younger man's hand. "I won't consider myself successful until I actually succeed in making you switch your opinions, dear fellow."

"I take it Mr. Stone is a new member of Commons," Caroline said. She was surprised that he could have met the minimum age of one-and-twenty to be in the House of Commons, but she would not voice her opinion for fear of embarrassing him.

"Indeed, and this is the first time I've actually been face to face with The Great Orator," Mr. Stone said.

"Who, pray tell, is The Great Orator?" Lady Harriett asked.

Lady Harriett needed to learn not to ask questions that would point to her own ignorance. Caroline made eye contact with her charge and casually wiped a hand across her brow.

Lady Harriett nodded almost imperceptivity.

Mr. Stone turned to the lady. "That's what we in the House

of Commons call Mr. Muir."

"A pity I'm not as well informed as Miss Rutherford," Lady Harriett said.

"But," Caroline intervened, "Lady Harriett has expressed an interest in learning more about Parliament."

"A good plan, especially considering her brother is a force in the House of Lords," Viscount Hewitt said.

Lady Harriett gave an exasperated look. "I do know that."

Mr. Muir exchanged pleasantries before he sat down and faced the ladies' sofa.

"Did you know Miss Rutherford is uncommonly well informed about what's going on in Parliament?" Mr. Muir asked his companions.

His comment resulted in all their gazes locking on Caroline and in her feeling uncomfortable with the attention. Why was it her passion always drew such a high level of interest? Were she passionate about drawing, for instance, no one would be gawking at her as they were now.

To her delight and Lady Harriett's consternation the group spent the next half-hour discussing pending legislation. Then, in accordance with the rules of paying calls, the gentlemen took their leave before they could abuse their welcome, but they agreed to see one another again the following night at Almack's.

"By the by," Viscount Hewitt said before leaving, "I'd like to arrange an expedition to the museum at Montague House for us to see the Rosetta Stone."

Movement in the doorway caught Caroline's attention. She turned and saw Lord Devere standing there. "I should enjoy being one of the group," he said.

Then nothing could keep Caroline from going to the museum.

They set the date for two days hence.

HE AND ALEX sat on one side of the barouche facing Harriett and Miss Rutherford. Devere wanted to compliment Miss Rutherford on how fetching she looked in her new frock of muslin sprigged with lavender flowers, but he did not want to call her to Alex's attention. The man was entirely too besotted over her.

The previous night at Almack's, Alex had danced with no one but her. Exactly as Devere himself had done. He'd never seen Alex act like this before over any female, and they'd been close friends since they were lads at Eton.

Even though he'd at first thought his friend and Miss Rutherford would be compatible, he had now changed his mind. For one thing, Alex understood that he needed to marry a well-dowered woman to bolster the family's eroding fortune. An up-and-coming Parliamentarian ought to be able to woo any number of wealthy maidens who would be in a position to help his career.

Serving his government had always been the guiding light of Alex's life. He needed at his side not just a woman who was knowledgeable about Parliament—as was Miss Rutherford. He especially needed more a woman whose wealth and family would be in a position to advance his career. Alex was destined to be First Lord.

Even if Alex thought he might want to align his future to Miss Rutherford's, he would later have regrets.

Devere was still surprising himself that he actually chose to spend his evening at Almack's.

"Have you been to Montague House before?" Alex asked Miss Rutherford.

"No. This will be my first visit, and I'm greatly looking forward to it."

In Bloomsbury, the trio of Harriett's admirers awaited them. Though they all vied for her attentions, Mr. Stone was even more eager to court Alex's favor. As soon as his group alighted from the barouche, young Stone latched on to Alex and began to pump him on matters of Parliament.

Which pleased Devere. He took the opportunity to begin

showing Miss Rutherford about the museum. "The viscount picked a good time to come," he told her, "because Montague House will soon be closing as the museum's to be relocated. There's no telling how long it will be before it opens again to the public."

Her hand rested on his proffered arm as she rolled her eyes. "I dare say they'll be building some showy facility to display the wretched Lord Elgin's marbles."

He watched her with amusement. When a topic drew her ire or her admiration, she forgot her shyness. "I believe your views on the subject must agree with own."

"Would that I could express myself as eloquently as Lord Byron. *Dull is the eye that will not weep to see thy walls defaced, thy mouldering shrines removed by British hands.*"

"It does make me ashamed of my country," he said, "that an important official of our government pillaged the country where he served."

"It's unconscionable to destroy structures that have stood thousands of years in order to bring the antiquities back to England—or Scotland, as the despicable Lord Elgin originally intended."

"It's almost as bad as what we and the French have done in Egypt," he said.

"Yet we're here today to get a glimpse of the fruits of their pillage."

He patted her hand. "It's refreshing to find a female whose opinions mirror my own."

She looked up at him and smiled to reveal teeth that were straight and white.

Though the stated purpose of today's visit was to see the Rosetta Stone, he did not want to share Miss Rutherford with their crowd of gawkers staring at the great find. He wanted to be the only one to stand with her when she saw it for the first time.

"Shall we save the Rosetta Stone for last?" he asked. "I thought we could look at some of the ancient manuscripts first."

"A good plan, my lord. Later, the crowds around the Rosetta Stone should diminish."

Had the lady invaded his thoughts?

As they strolled along the corridors, she came to a stop before a wall plaque. "I thought I saw your name!" Her gaze flicked from the plaque to him. "Why did you not tell me you were a trustee here?"

He shrugged. "My father was instrumental in the museum's earlier days. I'm merely attempting to carry on with what he started."

"I think that's very noble."

Possessing her good opinion mattered.

"Since you, my lord, are a trustee, please tell me why the Rosetta Stone is on display to the public when scholars are still in the process of unlocking its mysteries."

"That's easy to answer. Rubbings have been made of the stone, and it's the rubbings that are being studied by the scholars."

They were the only occupants of the first manuscript room they came to. Her hand continued to rest on his arm as they made their way around the chamber. "I suppose you would have been raised around books since your father was a learned clergyman," he said.

She did not respond for a moment. Why was it whenever he asked her a personal question, she always hesitated before answering? "Yes. There were always books about," she finally answered.

"I don't suppose he would have expected a daughter to learn Latin?"

She gave a little laugh. "No, I never learned Latin."

"But my sister says your French is very good."

"Is that not a prerequisite for my position in your household?"

His step slowed to a stop. "You're not to speak of your *position*. What have I told you since that first afternoon?"

She swallowed. Her lashes lowered. Her voice dropped. "I'm to be treated as a member of the Beresford family."

Once again, she looked utterly vulnerable. And desirable. He moved closer and settled his hands at her waist as his head lowered and his lips softly pressed into hers. He had not thought about what he was doing or what the lady's reaction would be. He'd acted purely on unprecedented feelings. Which was completely out of character.

His first glimmer of cognizant thought was his expectation that the incensed lady would push him away.

But nothing could be further from the reality. She made no effort to break away. She clung to him like wet leaves, her breathing uneven, her body trembling. Her kiss was everything he could ever have hoped for: sweet, delicate, potent.

And he did not want it to end.

Then he heard footsteps in the corridor. Reluctantly, he broke the kiss—but not the connection. He tenderly peered down at her and whispered. "I should beg your forgiveness, but I could never regret what just happened."

She spoke in a breathless whisper. "I pray, my lord, you not take me for a strumpet."

He looked into her face. Such elemental purity he'd never seen. "It would be easier to think Westminster Abbey a country chapel."

Harriett and the four other fellows came barreling into the manuscript room. "Why did you not come see the Rosetta Stone?" his sister asked. "What an epic find it's been!"

"I wish to see it when the chamber's less crowded," he answered.

"Then you ought to go now," Alex said. "I'll come with you."

This was one time Devere did not want to be with his closest friend.

AFTER THE UNSAVORY men in his employ had learned that Charlotte Robinson had come to Betsy Wyndham from Cheshire, they traveled to that county and encountered no difficulty in discovering what there was to know about the lady. Unfortunately, she was the only Robinson left, so there were no relatives with whom she could now communicate. A pity.

He had learned that she had spent a great deal of time in London. Surely that's where her trail would terminate. After all, it was a large city in which to get lost. And he had the advantage that he knew of her existence, but she didn't know his.

Unless she possessed Betsy's book—and that was very likely.

It was imperative that he find her. Dare he hope she was still using her real name?

CHAPTER SIX

"I must own," Lady Harriett said in the barouche on the way home from the museum, "I am excessively enjoying the attentions from three highly eligible men. But I do declare, it's difficult to choose."

"You don't have to choose now," her brother said. "Nor do you have to make a commitment this Season. I believe our sisters heartily recommend waiting until one is absolutely certain."

Caroline looked from brother to sister and nodded. Lady Harriett needed no guidance from her when her own brother exercised such sound judgment.

"Just going by appearances," Lady Harriett rattled on, "Mr. Pring would win my affections. Do you not find him massively handsome, Miss Rutherford?"

"Was I supposed to be judging them in such a manner?" Caroline answered playfully.

"How could you not be aware of those deep blue eyes and that coal black hair?" Lady Harriett asked.

For the very good reason that Caroline had eyes only for one man. The memory of being kissed by Lord Devere still had the power to accelerate her heartbeat. Just sitting across from him on this breezy, sunny summer day suffused her with a deep sense of well-being.

Her cheeks stung when she recalled her wanton response to

his lordship's touch. Even though she was embarrassed over how greedily she had kissed him back, had she to do it all over again, she would not have hesitated to repeat the enthusiasm of her kiss.

How could she have fallen so completely under his drugging spell when she'd known him but for five days? And it wasn't as if anything could ever come of her deep attachment to him. They were of two different worlds, and she did not belong in his.

"Of course," Lady Harriett continued, "Mr. Stone is exceedingly serious about his parliamentary duties. I predict he will go far, and I do find that admirable."

"You're right, Bitsy," Mr. Muir said, "that young man will go far. He's got a bright future. You could do far worse."

Lord Devere glared at his friend. "Pray, Muir, don't be encouraging my sister to plight her life with any man just yet. She's young and in no hurry."

Undeterred by the men in the carriage, Lady Harriett went on as if she were thinking aloud. "And I cannot discount Lord Hewett. Our papas were dear friends, and I would adore being mistress of Abingdon House."

Caroline shook her head ruefully while wiping her brow.

Lady Harriett giggled. "Do you know when Miss Rutherford wipes her brow it is to encourage me to cease talking nonsense."

Lord Devere regarded Caroline with amusement. "It happens that I'm in agreement with Miss Rutherford. One does not speak of selecting a life's mate based on his family's residence."

"To be sure," Mr. Muir agreed. "I might also suggest, Bitsy, you assure yourself your future mate not be averse to those creatures with which you surround yourself."

Caroline's eyes widened as she peered at Mr. Muir. "Bitsy?"

He shrugged. "I've known the lady since she was a toddler."

The lady smiled upon him. "Alex has always called me Bitsy."

Alex? Smiling, Caroline swiped her brow.

"Oh, dear me, I'm not to call you Alex, Mr. Muir. It's entirely too familiar, and as you know, I'm not a child anymore."

"You don't even call your brother by his Christian name,"

Caroline said, shooting a glance at his lordship. She had no idea what his Christian name was.

"Nobody calls him Henry," Lady Harriett said.

Caroline and Devere's gazes locked. She swallowed. Just thinking of calling him Henry intoxicated her. How fortunate would be the woman who would one day be that close to him.

"I inherited at a fairly young age," he explained. "It's hard to remember when I wasn't referred to as Devere."

"Oh, Devere," his sister said, "Miss Rutherford and I will go to the Duke of Bedford's ball tonight. Will you come?"

His gaze once more moved to Caroline. "How can I resist the opportunity to dance with Miss Rutherford again?"

"A pity I cannot come," Mr. Muir said. "I must dine at the Hollands' tonight."

"Oh, to be a fly on that wall," Caroline said. Her father used to participate in the lively political dinners at Holland House.

"You must come one night," Mr. Muir said to her.

"Yes," Devere echoed. "I shall take you myself."

Mr. Muir did not look amused.

"Nothing could give me more pleasure," Caroline said. *Except kissing him again.*

They arrived back at Devere House, and she was disappointed their trip was being terminated.

MISS RUTHERFORD'S PRESENCE in his house these past two weeks had destroyed his former routine of spending every night at White's. Why was it Devere was suddenly enjoying all the activities he'd shunned the past decade? During the last fortnight, he'd accompanied that lady and his sister to half a dozen balls, gone to Almack's twice, taken a day trip to the British Museum, and had twice gone to the theatre. On the nights when there had been no planned activities, he and Alex made a foursome with the ladies at whist.

He was well aware that he craved every minute in the lady's company, but he was at a loss to explain why a bashful woman without dazzling beauty could have so entrapped him. It wasn't as if she flirted. Quite the contrary.

Not once since the day he'd kissed her at the museum had the opportunity presented itself for a repeat of that most satisfying occurrence. How he longed to take her in his arms and kiss her again. He thought about it day and night.

He thought, too, of her words that day. *I pray, my lord, you not take me for a strumpet.* Did she think because she was in a subservient position that he would try to take advantage of her? As much as he desired her, he cared too much to ever compromise her virtue. And he had no doubts as to her virtue.

His heart went out to young women of good birth whose circumstances forced them into situations that could lead to degradation by unfeeling masters.

During these past weeks they had enjoyed several discussions about Parliament. It was the only time she allowed her speech to flow naturally. He knew how much she would enjoy sitting at the Holland House table surrounded by the most influential people in government.

He waited until a night he knew Alex would be otherwise occupied to invite her to accompany him to the Hollands' Kensington establishment. He was half-ashamed of the way he kept angling to exclude his best friend, but he loathed the idea of sharing Miss Rutherford with Alex.

It was a night, too, in which she was duty free, owing to the fact Harriett cancelled all obligations because of a persistent headache.

At first, Miss Rutherford was reluctant to leave Harriett but agreed to do so after his sister assured her that she would send word to Holland House if she had any kind of setback.

It was still light outside as he and Miss Rutherford rode the considerable distance to Kensington. He'd often wondered, given the congestion on these London streets, why Lord Holland persisted in living so far away from the Palace of Westminster, a place where he spent so much of his time during Parliamentary sessions.

As Devere peered across the carriage, he found himself wondering if any of the men at tonight's dinner would be as affected by Miss Rutherford's quiet charm as he. There was nothing about her dress that could ever be construed as attention-grabbing. Even its color of ivory was as bland as this morning's porridge.

Were he asked to analyze which of the lady's attributes had so captivated him, he would have been powerless to do so. There was no single distinguishing feature but rather a satisfying compendium of attractions ranging from a pleasing figure to sound judgment and an acute understanding of all things political. Miss Rutherford looked like a woman—an attractive woman— and thought like a man.

"How old were you when you first came to Holland House?" she asked.

"I was fortunate to be invited the first year I served in the House of Lords. Why do you ask?"

"I suppose I was wondering if you ever had the honor of meeting Lord Holland's famed uncle."

"Would that I had," he said ruefully. "The closest I ever came was the day I was privileged to hear the great Charles James Fox speak on the floor of the House of Commons when I visited at the age of eighteen."

"Do you agree he was one of the finest speakers ever?"

"He was remarkably effective, but I wouldn't want to discount Pitt—even if he was on the *other side*. Tell me how it is you could know so much about a man who's been dead for nearly a decade?"

She did not answer for a moment. "As you know, I've always been keenly interested in the workings of government."

"Your clergyman father shared your enthusiasm?"

"You say this because you believe a clergyman's time is spent preparing sermons and tutoring lads in the classics in order to provide for their families?" Her eyes flashed with mirth.

"Yes. I find it surprising your father would have had time to so thoroughly understand matters of government."

Instead of making a response, she lifted the coach's velvet curtain and peered at the buildings they swept past. Why was it queries about her father always resulted in muteness? He had the distinct feeling she was hiding something from him.

Shortly after they arrived at Holland House, the thirty visitors were shown into the dinner room. Miss Rutherford was paired with a low-ranking member of the House of Commons while he, because of his rank as an earl, sat immediately to Lady Holland's right.

He hoped Miss Rutherford would not feel as if she were a fish out of water. He knew that intellectually she was a match for anyone at the table, but would she feel an interloper because of her humble background? Perhaps bringing her tonight wasn't serving her best interests. He would rather engage in a duel to the death than to hurt her in any way.

His fears for her well-being were quickly answered. He could tell she was loving every minute by the way her head swiveled from side to side as she eagerly watched the speakers and by the way the corners of her mouth lifted and her eyes sparkled.

Her shyness prevented her from adding to the conversation, even though she would have sagely contributed to the topic being discussed, that of penal reform, a matter upon which she had expounded her opinions to him—opinions that were very similar to his own.

"While we're on the subject of penal reform," Lord Holland said, "I'd like to gauge interest in the English adopting some sort of well-defined system of ... to borrow a word from the French, *police*. It's senseless that a metropolis like London has absolutely no governmental authority to deal with crime."

"The French system of policing has significantly reduced crime," Lady Holland said.

Devere smiled at her. "This is a rare occasion when I'm inclined to agree with an arch Francophile like you, my lady."

"But Englishmen will never approve of armed law enforcement," Mr. Russell said. "It's too militaristic."

Devere nodded. "I agree. They would have to be for the people, of the people."

"And," Lord Holland added, "the time has come to have professional, paid law enforcement."

Lady Holland sighed. "I wonder if it will come in our lifetime."

Her husband smiled. "It will."

It did not escape his notice that the gentleman who'd escorted her to the table could not seem to remove his eyes from Miss Rutherford. "Tell me your name again," that gentleman said.

"Char . . . er, Caroline Rutherford."

Why, Devere wondered, had she almost called herself by another name? He became more convinced that she was hiding something from him.

"And you, Mr. Keynes, have just been successful in your electioneering efforts, have you not?" she asked.

Devere was remarkably impressed over her knowledge of Parliament. He, who read all the newspapers daily, did not know of Mr. Keynes' election.

"Indeed, Miss Rutherford. I stood for Maidenhead," Keynes said.

"How are you liking sitting in the House of Commons?"

The young man chuckled. "I'd be lying if I said I wasn't intimidated."

She offered him a smile. "I dare say that's to be expected and will quickly pass once you get your sea legs, so to speak. You are a Whig?"

"I wouldn't be here at Lord Holland's were I not."

"I suppose I should have known that," she said.

"Where," Lady Holland asked Devere, "is your friend Mr. Muir tonight?"

"I believe he was committed to taking his sister to the theatre.

I assure you, he'd much rather be here."

"The man is terribly passionate about his Parliamentary duties."

"Indeed." A pity Alex was so much older than Harriett for he possessed the qualities Devere would hope for in his sister's future husband. He sighed. Unfortunately, Harriett only had eyes for men close to her own youthful age.

"You and Mr. Muir must come here next week," Lady Holland said. "It will be our honor to host Madame de Staël." He would rather come with Miss Rutherford than with Alex.

It did not escape Devere's notice that Lord Holland rolled his eyes. "I'm surprised," jolly Lord Holland said, "my wife will have the woman."

"Why is that?" Devere asked.

"Much to my chagrin, my wife has always been enamored of Napoleon, and Napoleon detested Madame de Staël."

"Then the rest of us will be happy to welcome Madame de Staël," John Russell said with a laugh.

Devere directed his remarks to Miss Rutherford. "The Hollands not only surround themselves with government officials, they also enjoy the company of great writers and artists."

"I have read about their dinners for many years," Miss Rutherford said, "and am honored to be able to experience one."

During the dinner, Devere had noticed that Sir Andrew Wittingham had been staring at Miss Rutherford, and as the sweetmeats were being laid, he finally spoke to her. "Where have we met before, Miss Rutherford?"

She froze and ever so slowly made eye contact with the elderly man. "I'm sure I would have remembered it if I had met a man of your stature before but, alas, Sir Andrew, I'm a newcomer to London."

The older man, who'd spent several decades in powerful positions in the House of Commons, shook his head. "I never forget a face. It will come to me."

Miss Rutherford stiffened and turned her attention to her

plate. It was unlike her not to be gracious.

It had been weeks since Devere had enjoyed himself as much as he did that night. He not only enjoyed talking politics with a like-minded group of men from the highest levels of government, but he also derived great joy from watching Miss Rutherford's almost childlike appreciation of the conversation and the opportunity to mingle with these officials.

After Sir Andrew spoke to her, Miss Rutherford's demeanor changed. Thereafter, she was sullen and silent.

In the coach on the way home, her enthusiasm returned. "To think, all the Whig grandees in one chamber, and I got to be there! Thank you for inviting me."

"It's obvious, my dear Miss Rutherford, you hold no love for Tories."

"Oh, dear, is it that obvious?"

"Indeed it is. Would you even have come to my house were I a Tory?"

Her voice turned serious. "One in my position has not the luxury of totally free choice."

Which made him think of the unfortunate young women who were taken advantage of by the men who employed them. Some of the women were clergymen's daughters, like Miss Rutherford. It was disgusting.

"It looked as if you were getting along nicely with Mr. Keynes."

"Do you not think he would be a good match for Lady Harri-ett?"

"I thought the man might be interested in you."

"But he's younger than me." She said it as if she were questioning Devere's sanity.

Then she was not interested in her dinner companion. "He's a great deal closer to your age than . . . Mr. Muir." *Or me.*

She shook her head. "Mr. Muir is a dear man, but we are nothing more than friends."

Why in the devil did that intelligence relieve him? That and her disinterest in Richard Keynes.

He almost brought up Sir Andrew, but he had no desire to make her uncomfortable, and for some reason, she was uncomfortable around that aged politician.

"You were really in your element tonight," he said.

"I don't know when I've ever had a more pleasant evening in my life." She paused, biting her lip. "No woman in my position has ever had a better situation than I've come to at Devere House."

It was a moment before he could respond. "My sister is very dear to me, and you, Miss Rutherford, have been very good for my sister. It's we who are fortunate."

The remainder of the ride home passed in silence, the only noise the clop of hooves on the city's dark streets. Without being overt, he stared at her. How he wanted to move to her side of the coach and draw her into his arms once again.

He'd had no right to kiss her that day at the museum, nor could he allow himself to repeat the action.

No matter how pleasant it had been.

As LONG AS Miss Charlotte Robinson drew breath, his own neck was in danger. Her knowledge of his crime could send him to the gallows. It had taken two weeks for his faithful—though thoroughly disreputable—henchmen to investigate the young woman's background, and they were about to apprise him of what they'd learned.

He remained seated behind the desk in his library as the two entered his chamber, their clothing still bearing the unmistakable signs of the dusty roads they'd traveled. As distasteful as it was to even have them in his house, he invited them to take a seat in front of him.

He could barely contain his eagerness. "Have you found her?"

The men had orders to kill her—a service for which they would be handsomely rewarded. But not until they had taken possession of the journal.

Johnson, a fifty-year-old man with ruddy complexion and ill-fitting clothing, ruefully shook his head.

"But," his companion, Goddard, added, "we can explain why it is that she's got no home to return to from Devon." A bit younger than his companion, Goddard was equally as ill dressed. The sooner the misfits were gone from his home, the better. He'd rather not be seen with the likes of them.

"Then bloody well tell me why."

"She's got no home no more," Johnson said.

"I could have surmised a similar account, owing to the fact she went into service for Mrs. Wyndham," he snapped. Still, he was curious about her.

Johnson looked wounded, but went on nevertheless. "Her father, one Matthew Robinson, was apparently a man of significant social standing."

The name Matthew Robinson was familiar to him.

Goddard nodded enthusiastically. "He was a member of Parliament. A Whig."

"*Was?*" he asked, his eyes widening.

Both men nodded.

"He was killed in a fire," Johnson said.

Now he remembered reading about the tragedy in the newspapers.

Goddard nodded. "And his son with him. We learned that Miss Robinson was in London at the time. That's how she escaped the deadly fire."

"The fire destroyed their house, and we were told it had been a fine house, the finest house in Romford-on-Mersey."

"In Birmingham?"

Both men shook their heads. "No. In Cheshire," Johnson answered. "Name of the village is Romford-on-Mersey." Johnson was the one who always dealt directly with him. He'd been engaging the man's nefarious services for nearly two decades.

"We asked around," Goddard said, "and no one anywhere around Romford-on-Mersey has heard from the lady since she lost everyone and everything in the fire. It weren't long after that she arrived at Betsy Wyndham's."

As disappointing as it was that she'd not returned to her home, he understood. She had nothing to return to. Not only had she lost her family, the family's home and fortune must have been lost in the fire, or else she would not have been forced to go into service. "Did you get a good description of Charlotte Robinson?" he asked.

"The best we could," Johnson said.

Goddard nodded in agreement.

"She was somewhere between the age of twenty and five-and-twenty. Those both in Devon and in Romford-on-Mersey said she was a handsome girl. Girl is the word they used to describe her, though I dare say I wouldn't call one who's five-and-twenty a girl. She was said to be somewhat ordinary looking with a figure that was described as average, and her hair was described as being a medium brown. No one could say what color her eyes were, except to say they weren't dark."

At least he now had something to go on. "That's all I'll need from you at this time," he said, opening his desk drawer, withdrawing two pouches of coins, and tossing them to the pair. "I'll be getting in touch when I learn more."

If Charlotte Robinson wasn't in Devon or in Cheshire, there was a good likelihood she had come to London. He suspected she had at least one friend here in the Capital. Her father had served in Parliament; therefore the family must have spent a few months each year in London.

It was perfectly natural that she would return here.

He knew now where to look for Miss Charlotte Robinson.

CHAPTER SEVEN

DURING THE YEARS he'd engaged employees from Miss Fletcher's Domestic Assistance Agency for Discriminating Employers, Devere never had reason to complain. The woman did an exemplary job in furnishing professionals of the highest quality. Miss Rutherford was no exception. But as qualified as she was, he was plagued with doubts as to the veracity of her background.

He was consumed by guilt for doubting her. She had proven to be more than competent in every way and was a credit to the high standards Miss Fletcher maintained. He felt ashamed for questioning the lady's references.

What could be accomplished by digging into Miss Rutherford's past? Would it really matter to the performance of her duties? She was doing a wonderful job with Harriett. Moreover, Harriett genuinely enjoyed the lady's companionship.

So why in the devil was he so intent on answering these questions that dominated his thoughts? If there were a secret from her past, would it reflect unfavorably on her performance with his sister? What could she possibly have done that would render her unfit to be with his sister? He would never believe her culpable of any infraction that would disqualify her from serving in their home.

So it boiled down to his own burgeoning doubts. It was for his own sake he needed to know more about this woman whose quiet presence, in so many ways, had come to shake his world.

The morning after they dined at the Hollands', he summoned his man of business. Timothy Eardley, dressed as finely as any gentleman at White's, strolled into Devere's library, cheerfully greeting the man he had served for the past decade. After pleasantries were exchanged, the two sat in armchairs near the tall casement where the royal blue draperies had been opened to flood the chamber with sunlight.

"I have an undertaking for you," Devere began. "It's imperative that this undertaking is conducted with the utmost discretion. Word of it can never reach those who inhabit this house."

"Of course, my lord." Eardley gave his employer a quizzing look. Even ten years earlier, when he was just in his mid-twenties, the solicitor had demonstrated uncommon capabilities.

Eardley never disappointed. His duties had ranged from drawing up Devere's will to investigating the ownership of land Devere wished to acquire adjacent to Hamberly. Devere had never presented a problem Eardley had failed to solve.

"I wish for you to investigate the origins of my sister's companion, Miss Caroline Rutherford. We've been uncommonly pleased with the lady, yet I feel as if she's hiding something from us, something about her past."

Devere found himself wondering if anything Eardley might unearth would change his high opinion of the lady or could possibly cause him to dismiss her. He doubted it. Nevertheless, his own curiosity demanded to be satisfied.

"She came to you from Miss Fletcher's?" Since Eardley paid all his accounts, he knew as much about running Devere's household as Devere himself. Perhaps more.

"She did, and Miss Fletcher has never disappointed. I should add that my sister has also found Miss Rutherford to be exemplary."

Eardley nodded. "Tell me what you know of her past."

"What I know and what it actually is may be two different matters. I don't know why I feel it so strongly, but I have an acute conviction that her background has been fabricated."

"How so?"

"That's what you're to tell me."

"Tell me what was presented to you. It will be my job to prove it or to disprove it." Eardley withdrew a small notebook from his pocket with which to take notes.

Exactly what Devere wanted. "The lady claims to come to us from Shropshire where she served as companion to one Mrs. Smythe-Higgins, now deceased."

Eardley raised a brow.

"Before that," Devere continued, "Miss Rutherford claims to have been one of a large progeny of a Shropshire clergyman. Apparently, her father's parish changed with regularity." Both the death of the former employer and the fact her family had no roots raised red flags.

Eardley wrote in his notebook while nodding. "Would you mind telling me why you have reason not to believe her?"

Devere did not answer for a moment. It was difficult to articulate his doubts. "Nothing solid, just little things. She's reluctant to speak of her father. She's never mentioned a single sibling. And once, she almost referred to herself by another name." He drew his breath. "And she claimed to have never met Sir Andrew Wittingham though he seemed certain he had met her before."

He frowned before continuing, hoping he didn't sound stupid. "There's one more thing. She has a passionate interest in politics which I find perplexing for one who has spent the whole of her life buried in Shropshire."

Eardley nodded. "And for a female, at that." The solicitor stood. "It could take me up to a month to conduct this investigation, my lord."

"I wouldn't have expected anything less." Devere's fondest wish was that Eardley would come back from Shropshire with evidence that Caroline Rutherford was, indeed, who she said she was.

⇶⇷

"WHAT, MIGHT I ask, are you reading this morning?" Caroline inquired with levity as she walked into Lady Harriett's sunny study. It was a rare occurrence, indeed, to see that lady read anything other than fashion books and gossip columns.

Before the lady could set down her newspaper, the orange cat on her lap started stabbing at it with her—or his—paw. Lady Harriett tossed the cat onto the carpet. "It's exceedingly difficult to read the newspaper with Pumpkin on my lap."

"If you were truly serious about reading your morning paper, might I suggest not having a feline on your lap? It wouldn't hurt to shut the door of your study to give yourself some private time with the news."

Lady Harriett's brows lowered. "I hate to hurt my kitties' feelings."

"I believe their short-term memories are so inexact they won't be able to ascertain for how long you've shut them out. To them, it may only seem to have been a single minute."

"You're so wise."

"Shall I put Pumpkin in your bedchamber? Then he'll be mad at me and not you."

"She. Pumpkin's a she, and yes, do banish the poor thing."

After removing the cat, Caroline came to sit, facing Lady Harriett who was already dressed for the day in a pale blue muslin dress. She looked lovely—and hardly older than sixteen. "When did you begin to be interested in the *Morning Chronicle*?"

"Today's my first day, and I'm finding it exceedingly interesting. It's rather exciting to know the important people mentioned here."

"Like Alex Muir?"

"Yes."

"I thought you found such reading dull."

"I've made some decisions about my life," Lady Harriett

announced with the air of a seasoned matriarch.

"And?"

"And I've decided you and my brother were right. About Lord Hewitt. Being attracted to him because he's the owner of Abingdon House is a very poor reason to consider marriage."

"Does this . . ." Caroline indicated the *Morning Chronicle*. "Mean that you're developing an interest in politics because you've decided upon Mr. Stone?"

"Oh, dear me, no. You know Mr. Stone is a Tory. While my knowledge of politics is sadly lacking, I could never cast my affections at one who so disagreed with my brother. Or with Mr. Muir."

Caroline smiled. "I'm delighted to see you taking an interest in matters of government. Your brother will be, too. As you become better informed, you will come to understand how important your brother is."

The lady got up and went to Mr. Mousie's house, unlatched it, and removed the creature. While squeezing it firmly, she pressed her lips to his pelt and murmured endearments to the creature Caroline found loathsome. "I've never doubted Devere," Lady Harriett said.

Who could? Caroline wished she wasn't so fiercely attracted to the man, but who wouldn't be? He was perfection. "You're showing uncommonly sound judgment. Your brother will be proud."

Lady Harriett was beginning to show maturity—even if she did adopt the most peculiar pets. "So, in spite of being a member of the House of Commons, Mr. Stone is not the man for you?"

"That's exactly what I've decided."

"So you've also eliminated Lord Hewitt and Mr. Stone. What of Mr. Pring?"

"I tried to think of myself as Lady Harriett Pring, but I could never accept such a silly name—even though he is excessively handsome."

Caroline looked sternly at her charge.

"But that's not the only reason I cannot align myself with Mr. Pring." She shrugged her shoulders. "He just doesn't appeal to me."

"I think you're demonstrating wisdom. As your brother keeps reminding you, you're under no compulsion to find a husband this year."

"Lord Wetherspoon's going to call on me today. Perhaps he will be The One. Did you not think him utterly handsome?"

Next to the lady's brother, all other men were woefully inadequate. Caroline had noticed little about Lord Wetherspoon, except that he was a bit older than the lady's other admirers. He was probably Caroline's own age. Other than that singular observation, Caroline had scarcely paid any attention to him. "It's not my opinion that matters. However, if I find a man not deserving of your affections, be assured I will apprise you of it."

"I am greatly looking forward to going to Vauxhall Gardens tonight. Perhaps I shall even expand my circle of admirers."

Because Caroline had never been to Vauxhall, apprehension of the unknown seized her, stealing her customary confidence. "Have you been before?" Perhaps Lady Harriett could orient her before they went.

"No. This will be my first time, and I'm vastly looking forward to it."

"The only thing I've ever heard about the gardens is worrisome—and of course I've read Fanny Burney's *Evelina*."

Lady Harriett nodded. "There is that. One cannot forbid disreputable people from paying their shilling to attend, but since Devere will be with us, we have no worries."

Hope blossomed in Caroline's breast. "Then your brother will be coming?"

"He is. In fact, he's said I'm not permitted to go there ever without him. My trio of admirers—even though I no longer favor them—will come, and I shall ask Lord Wetherspoon to also meet us there."

"Four suitors all at once? You'll be the envy of every lady

there."

DEVERE AND ALEX faced the ladies in the carriage as it sped toward Vauxhall that night. To Devere's chagrin, Alex had invited himself to accompany them.

The tensions between the two men had been running high since Miss Rutherford had begun her employment in his home. As determined as Devere was not to allow a woman to come between him and his closest friend, he needed to make Alex understand that a union with Miss Rutherford would do him irreparable harm. He needed to speak bluntly to Alex. But not tonight.

Was Devere spending so much time with Miss Rutherford to keep her from ruining Alex? He could not lie to himself. His interest in Miss Rutherford had nothing to do with his best friend.

"You ladies look lovely tonight." Alex looked at Miss Rutherford as he spoke.

It was as if Alex had stolen the words off Devere's tongue. He, too, had been unable to remove his gaze from his sister's companion. If he was not mistaken, she was wearing that same green dress she'd worn when the mouse frightened her up that chair in Harry's dressing room, the dress that was his sister's. The memory of the incident had him smiling.

Seeing how lovely Miss Rutherford was in the green dress must have compelled Harriett to gift it to the lady. As pretty as his sister was, she could never have looked as lovely in this dress that matched the shimmering green of Miss Rutherford's eyes.

And Harriett could never have filled out the dress' bodice so enticingly.

As their vehicle neared the gardens, he took pleasure in watching the ladies' reactions when they first beheld the abundant lights and Oriental lanterns that swung over the gardens and illuminated the towering stage in the distance.

Miss Rutherford's gaze met his. "It's quite lovely."

"Wait until you see the fireworks. It's all rather magical," he said.

After disembarking, he led them through the garden's wide main path. Progression was slow, owing to the throngs of pleasure seekers pushing their way toward the more brightly lit entertainment pavilion. The closer they came to it, the louder the orchestra music. The festive mood of their fellow attendees dressed in fancy attire and the melodic strains from the musicians accounted for the lightness in his step as they approached the classically styled building where they were to dine.

His sister's admirers—four of them—awaited their foursome there. The eight of them were shown to a cozy booth large enough to accommodate all eight of them. While Harriett found herself surrounded by her bevy of admirers, it happened that he sat on Miss Rutherford's right, and Alex managed to sit at her left.

This was actually his first opportunity to observe Harriett's suitors in a conversational setting. All of them were worthy men, thank God. But after conversing with them a good bit, he couldn't seem to warm to any of them. Perhaps it was their youth that rendered them so dull.

He watched his sister to see if he could detect any partiality, but he was not able to discern any preference on her part, nor did she exhibit any great enthusiasm toward a single one of the men.

But what did he know? He had little experience with affairs of the heart.

He lowered his voice so Harriett and her admirers would not be able to hear as he spoke to Miss Rutherford. "Do you find my sister has bestowed her affections on any of these fellows?" She would know far better than he.

"I don't believe she has," she answered in an equally low voice.

The two of them then directed their attention at the young lady being discussed. Harriett might not be falling in love with any of the four, but she was obviously enjoying being courted by so many worthy gentlemen.

Her pale eyes sparkled as she spoke with flirtatious coyness. "I declare, Mr. Stone, you are so knowledgeable about absolutely everything."

After bestowing her attentions on Stone, she directed her attentions to Lord Wetherspoon. "I dare say you must be acquainted with my brother since you sit in the House of Lords."

Lord Wetherspoon's reverent gaze darted to Devere, and a smile lifted as he nodded at the brother of the lady he was wooing. "It's my honor to be slightly acquainted with his lordship."

Slightly was an apt description. The young rake only rarely showed his face in the House of Lords—much like Devere when he was the same age. Too much pleasure seeking. Devere nodded at the fellow.

After supper, they gathered in front of the elevated orchestra stand to dance outdoors. Vauxhall was the one place where attendees were advised to dance only with members of their own party. To Devere's delight, Alex was not fond of dancing, so he had exclusive access to Miss Rutherford.

Alex was quickly besieged by fellow members of the House of Commons and became so engaged in conversation he neglected to stare at Miss Rutherford—a rare occurrence.

At the completion of their dance, Devere offered his dancing partner his crooked arm. "Shall we stroll in the garden? It's my duty to ensure that you get the full experience on your first visit here."

This once, he didn't mind leaving his maiden sister. With four devoted men paying her court, Devere had no worries about her well-being. And, besides, Alex was there. Good, staid, dependable Alex.

Miss Rutherford slipped her arm through his. Devere had not been prepared for how powerfully he would be affected by her closeness. He was reminded of his randy reaction to his first flirtation while a lad at Eton.

"From what I observed at dinner, my sister is a most practiced flirt," he said as they retraced the steps that had brought them here. Few were in the gardens now that the dancing had commenced.

Miss Rutherford let out a little laugh. "She is, but she's never unladylike, nor does she cross any line in regards to doing what's expected of a beautiful young lady of good breeding. To Lady Harriett's great consternation, none of those young men seem to be capable of winning her deep affection."

He chuckled. "Poor Harry. She so wants to be in love and to wed."

"Did you just refer to your sister as Harry?"

He chuckled. "Those in our family have always called her that. I try not to use that name around others, but sometimes I slip."

As they moved further away, the music faded. On nearly every intersecting path, muffled words between lovers carried on the balmy breezes that ruffled Miss Rutherford's locks. Beneath the lanterns, her hair sparkled as if threaded with gold.

They turned onto a little-used path, and he found himself even more profoundly affected by Miss Rutherford's nearness. He knew he should have avoided this dark, unused lane, but his desire for her was stronger than his integrity.

Not that he would ever compromise her.

But, damn, he craved her. He would go mad if he could not draw her into his arms and kiss her.

When the path terminated at a neatly clipped yew hedge, he stopped and took both her hands into his as he peered into her somber face. "I vow I will never take advantage of you, my dear Caroline, but I shall go mad if I can't kiss you."

She moved to him, so close her sweet rose scent clung to him like a pleasant dream lost too soon. Her head tilted upward, and her lips pressed to his.

CHAPTER EIGHT

As THE KISS deepened, his arms came around her. Her soft curves pressed to him, the fragrant rose scent of her, her throaty little whimper, the untamed way she responded to him all robbed him of rational thought. He could only feel. And, sweet heavens, what a feeling it was! The potency of their kiss nearly destroyed his composure.

It was as if the two were fusing into one. Where before, with other women, he'd been detached and unfeeling, this woman affected him like wind to wildfire, stoking his desire until it was raging out of control.

For her sake, not completely out of control.

How could a single kiss destroy his reserve so thoroughly? How could a man of two-and-thirty be so profoundly affected by a shy woman so vastly different from all the others he'd known? Perhaps that was her lure. Caroline Rutherford wasn't like those other women who'd never succeeded in capturing his heart.

When he heard voices coming closer, he reluctantly broke away. He cared too much for her to sully her reputation. She linked her arm to his as naturally as a babe suckles its mother's breast, and he covered her hand with his own as they strolled back down the shadowy path. The lilting strains of distant music completed the night's perfection.

With any other woman, he would have expected comments.

But not with Caroline. It would have to be up to him to try to address the magical blending that had just occurred between them.

From the way she'd so passionately kissed him, he knew that she felt this attachment as deeply as he did. "Please understand, I will never do anything that would hurt you or diminish my respect for you."

There was an unfamiliar breathlessness to her voice when she answered. "I know."

It was so simple a declaration but so much in character for this special woman who'd come to mean so much to him.

They returned to the area where revelers were dancing in front of the orchestra. Harriett was standing up with Lord Wetherspoon, a joyful look upon her delicate face.

Alex was still deep in conversation with his fellow members of the House of Commons, but not so deep that he neglected to notice Caroline. His face brightened when he saw her. He caught her gaze and nodded. Devere watched as she demurely returned the nod.

Then she looked up into Devere's face and spoke in a somber voice. "I beg that you not call me by my first name in front of others."

He squeezed her hand. "Tell me, Caroline," he said, his voice low and husky, "does it bother *you* when I call you by your Christian name?"

Their gazes held. He still felt that fusion to her. Finally, she shook her head. Without uttering a single word, she had confirmed this private bond between them. Feeling as if he'd grown a foot taller, he leaned into her. "I will claim you for a waltz."

CAROLINE HAD NEVER in her life behaved irrationally. She avoided snap decisions in favor of analyzing the situation from every perspective before adopting a stance. She never spoke before carefully considering each word she was going to say. She had certainly never before allowed her respectable self to head down a dark garden path with a man.

Yet ever since she'd met Lord Devere, it was as if another woman—a wanton one, at that—had invaded her mind and body. She didn't even know herself anymore.

Nothing in her five-and-twenty years had prepared her for the way Lord Devere affected her. She had not—even in those days when she was courted here in the Capital—ever been attracted to any man as she was to him. Even before that day when he'd first kissed her, she had found much in him to admire, and not just his rugged good looks. He was a caring brother, a considerate employer, a conscientious Parliamentarian. And he was a Whig.

Her previous apprehension over being taken advantage of by her privileged employer had dissipated because of his consideration for her feelings. She knew now he would never use her for his own pleasure. She understood that he was drawn to her in that same compelling way that made it impossible for her to deny him.

Since that day at the museum, she had been shocked that someone as ordinary as she could have attracted a man like Lord Devere. It seemed incomprehensible that he could possibly find in her something that would merit his consideration.

In the days that followed that kiss, everything she'd learned about him convinced her he had not acted merely upon impulse. He genuinely cared for her. He courted her opinions. He treated her with the same respect he would treat a family member. He shielded her reputation.

Never would she have thought she would allow any man to take such liberties with her. But with Lord Devere, those *liberties* were something to be cherished, something which she eagerly awaited and would always wish to repeat.

She was intelligent enough to know that she had no future

with a peer of the realm. When he married, he would be expected to wed a woman from his own class. She should protect her heart against being broken, but she was powerless to do so.

Just being with him was enough for her. Lord Devere had become as necessary to her happiness as air was to breathe.

There was also the matter of her untruthfulness. It would destroy any affection he held for her if he learned that she'd been lying to him about her identity since the day they had met.

As soon as the master of ceremonies announced the waltz, Mr. Muir abandoned his Parliamentary friends and headed toward her, but just before he joined them, Lord Devere claimed her for the shocking dance.

She failed to admit to him she had never waltzed before. She had observed enough of Lady Harriett's lessons with her dance master to be able to muddle through the set. Besides, being held in Lord Devere's arms would be like levitating on heavenly clouds.

During the dance, they weren't actually that close. They had been much closer when he'd held her in his arms and kissed her moments earlier. Now they were joined only by their hands, with several feet between their bodies.

But he drew her close, closer than many of the other couples, and murmured in her ear. "It occurs to me that holding you in my arms is much to my liking."

This once, she would allow herself to speak her heart. She could hold back no longer. "It pleases me, too."

"God, but it's hard to have you living under my roof."

She was thinking just the opposite, thinking how wonderful it was to see him every day. And every night.

Then she realized what he was referring to. He wanted to make love to her, but he was too noble, too much the gentleman, to act upon those feelings.

Never in her five-and-twenty years had she ever considered making love with any man. Until now. Her heart ached with want for this man, a want she could not permit herself to act upon.

She had no rank, no fortune, not even a family. She'd even lost her identity. All she had left was her self-respect, and she would cling to that.

"It would be easier, my lord, if we were just platonic friends." It grieved her say those words.

His step slowed, and he looked down at her. "Is that what you want, Caroline?"

She met his sultry gaze. Her eyes misted, and she shook her head.

He drew her closer.

After that dance, they enjoyed watching the dazzling fireworks display. Glorious bursts of color lighted the night sky, only to dissipate over the River Thames as if by magic. She found it mesmerizing. As was the man who'd brought her here. It was a magical night which would live on in her memory all the days and nights of her life.

Once the fireworks display was over, they made their way back to the Devere coach. In the carriage, she and Lady Harriett faced the men.

"Bitsy was certainly popular with the men tonight," Mr. Muir said. "Four of them were hovering around her like trout to minnows."

Lady Harriett preened. "It's vastly exciting, I do declare."

"I just want you to enjoy the Season," her brother said. "No one has ever said you must select a husband this year."

"I enjoy being courted but, alas, I can't seem to fix my affections upon any one man."

"So Lord Wetherspoon did not prove to be The One?" Caroline asked.

"I find much in him to admire, but my heart is not gushing with love for him. Sophia said I must wait until I meet the one man who's been created for me. She said I will know it because he will make my heart gush with love."

"Your sister is very wise," Mr. Muir said.

"You expected less of a Beresford?" Lord Devere teased. Then he directed his attention to his male companion. "Seriously, Muir, do you not believe that many men are deprived of free selection of a mate, owing to circumstances that compel them to marry for money?"

Mr. Muir did not immediately answer, and when he did, his voice was somber. "Sadly, my friend, you've hit the mark."

Did that mean that Mr. Muir was not wealthy, that he would have to marry an heiress? Caroline had always assumed that because he was Lord Devere's closest friend, Mr. Muir would also be plump in the purse.

"Many women, too, are denied a love match for the same reasons," Caroline said. She regretted her words as soon as she spoke. It wasn't her place to speak of things that did not pertain to Lady Harriett. She had made it a point not to talk about herself. It would be too easy to say something that would disclose her lies.

And what she'd just said definitely could be applied to her own circumstances. It was not likely Caroline would ever be able to marry for love, so she would stay a spinster who would always be forced to seek employment. Better that than subjecting herself to a loveless marriage.

"I suppose," Lady Harriett said, "I am most fortunate for I will not be obliged to wed for money. It's my good fortune that a handsome dowry has been bestowed upon me."

Yes, Lady Harriett was most fortunate, Caroline reflected. Not only did she have a dowry, but she had a family with siblings who obviously loved her.

Such thoughts, which quite naturally extended to Caroline's own lost loved ones, made her melancholy.

"That does *not* mean you'll be free to run off with a footman," Devere teased.

Lady Harriett defiantly lifted her chin. "I promised you I will never bestow my affections upon a man you deem unworthy, my dear brother."

Caroline adopted a didactic manner. "Since Mr. Muir is such a good friend who also happens to be on a familiar-name basis with Lady Harriett, I will remind Lady Harriett now, in front of him, that a lady should never bring up the subject of her dowry in front of a gentleman—as you just did with Mr. Muir."

"She's right, pet. And you're never to refer to your dowry outside of our immediate family." Devere turned to his friend. "Though, I will own, it seems like Alex is a member of our family."

"Indeed it does," Lady Harriett agreed.

His lordship's steady gaze went to Caroline. "And it goes without saying that we have no secrets from Miss Rutherford."

Caroline felt her cheeks stinging. She had secrets aplenty and, right now, she loathed her deception.

HE SAT IN the book-lined library of his Berkley Square mansion perusing the *Morning Chronicle*. The words he read caused him to sit up straight, excitement coursing through him. This was the first time since he'd killed Betsy Wyndham that he had hope of finding the young woman who could put a noose around his neck, the woman who had to be killed. But first, it was imperative he find Betsy's journal.

Knowing that Charlotte Robinson's father had been a prominent Whig, he'd pinned his hopes on the woman still maintaining those allegiances of her father's. And knowing that gatherings at Lord Holland's always featured prominent Whigs, he paid close attention to written accounts of those gatherings.

The night before last, a mysterious Miss Caroline Rutherford was among those in attendance at the Holland House gathering. Was it merely coincidence that her initials were the same as Charlotte Robinson's? It could be, but he thought not.

He based his assumption on the fact he'd never before seen a reference to Miss Caroline Rutherford, and he prized himself not only on being well informed on matters of government and goings-on among Society, but he also was possessed of a superior memory. Never before had Miss Caroline Rutherford's name graced the pages of the many London newspapers to which he subscribed.

He eagerly read the article, hoping to learn who accompanied Miss Rutherford to the dinner, but that information had been omitted.

He needed to find out from someone who had been at Holland House that night. This was obviously not a task for the crude likes of Johnson and Goddard.

He would have to find out himself.

CHAPTER NINE

LADY HARRIETT HAD a new suitor, one Richard Blythe-Corrington. Caroline thought he might have the edge over his competitors because he was a bit older than the other men who courted her and, therefore, had the potential to be more interesting. It did not detract from his appeal that he was possessed of healthy golden good looks and was said to have deep pockets.

This afternoon, he had collected the two ladies in his four-passenger barouche. Both females wore bonnets to protect their delicate skin from the sun as they paraded through bustling Hyde Park in his open vehicle on this warm summer day. Caroline noted that Blythe-Carrington's equipage was of considerably higher quality than others meandering along these paths—many of which accommodated just two passengers.

Caroline had attended enough balls, routs, and Almack's assemblies by now that she could recognize quite a few of the young ladies and gentlemen enjoying this warm afternoon in London's largest park. The first familiar face belonged to Mr. Davis, who nodded as he passed them in his phaeton. Moments later, Miss Emmott, accompanied by her friend, Miss Hardcastle, held the ribbons of a cabriolet which drew abreast of them. "Good day, Lady Harriett," Miss Emmott called out. "Miss Rutherford. It's a lovely day, is it not?"

Lady Harriett and Caroline agreed, just as Miss Hardcastle screeched as her horse became unmanageable, carrying them off at a brisk clip.

Pinks of the Ton in saddle horses mingled among them, along with groups of young ladies and their beaus casually strolling along the verdant paths, all dressed in stylish promenade wear.

Caroline would have enjoyed it more were Lord Devere with them, but the House of Lords was in session, and his duties always came first.

"Are you ladies fond of horses?" Mr. Blythe-Carrington asked.

"Miss Rutherford does not ride, if that's what you're asking," Lady Harriett responded. "I, on the other hand, adore riding."

Caroline's father had never seen fit to either keep a horse for his daughter or to provide her with riding lessons. She, therefore, maintained a hearty fear of climbing atop the beasts. Not being able to ride was never considered a hardship, owing to the fact her family spent more time in London than in Romford-on-Mersey.

"How I wish I could show you my stables at Wrentworth," he said. "They are accounted to be the finest in all of Somerset."

"Is it the facility that draws such admiration or the creatures that reside within them?" Lady Harriett asked. Caroline marveled that her companion never clammed up like she did in the company of gentlemen.

"It's my horses. I've got over two hundred, including two winners of the St. Leger."

"You have every right to be proud of them," Lady Harriett said. "As far as stables go, I was astonished over the magnificence of our regent's stables at Brighton. Have you seen them?"

"Only from the outside," he said.

"Me, too," Lady Harriett said. "Did you not find the regent's massive stables to be considerably more impressive than his Pavilion, which I find decidedly un-English with its pointed domes like something belonging to an Oriental potentate?"

He nodded. "I, too, prefer the stables over his Pavilion."

Lady Harriett turned to Caroline. "Have you been to Brighton, Miss Rutherford?"

"No, I haven't had that pleasure."

"Would it not be wonderful if I could persuade Devere to take us?"

"I doubt you'd succeed while Parliament meets. You know where your brother's priorities lie." Just another facet of him for Caroline to admire.

Lady Harriett's brows lowered, and her pretty face collapsed into a frown. "There is that."

"Lady Harriett has become interested in the workings of our government," Caroline told him. "She's been reading the accounts of Parliament every morning in the newspapers."

"Very commendable. Dare say I should give it a go myself. I'm more interested in reading the race reports myself. Anything to do with horses."

"I dare say you're one of those men who enjoys wagering on the race meetings," Lady Harriett said.

"You're bang on the mark, my lady."

It suddenly occurred to Caroline that Mr. Blythe-Carrington just might be dancing attendance upon Lady Harriett in order to get his hands on her dowry. Now that she was thinking on it, Caroline realized the gossip column in last week's *Tattler* alluded to the deep debts one Mr. R B-C had gotten himself into after the race meetings at Newmarket last month. That had to have been a reference to Mr. Richard Blythe-Carrington.

Lady Harriett was too tenderhearted and trusting. Caroline feared she would lose her heart to a blighter like him, and Caroline would do anything to protect her from so disastrous a match.

"I was wondering, Mr. Blythe-Carrington, if you are fond of animals," Lady Harriett said.

Oh, dear. Was Lady Harriett actually considering marriage to him? She always said the man she married had to love her pets.

"Indeed, I do. Can you not tell how exceedingly fond I am of horses?"

"I meant smaller animals. Like dogs and cats and other creatures for which one wants to provide a loving home."

"I, for one, would not feel compelled to provide a home for any small creatures unless they were dogs, and my mother, not being benevolent toward them, did not believe dogs should live indoors."

Caroline felt compelled to intervene. This was not the man for sweet Lady Harriett. "Lady Harriett is so enamored of pets she has actually nurtured a pet snake."

He shot a distasteful look at the lady being discussed. "Can't tolerate the slimy things. Give me a dog any day. I've got a wonderful bitch at Wrentworth who's the best mate a man could have in his shooting party."

"I beg you not to speak to me of shooting innocent animals," Lady Harriett said.

"Surely your brother shoots?"

"My brother no longer shoots. I was successful in persuading him to see how wicked a sport it is."

"Thought Devere had a better spine than that," he mumbled almost under his breath.

By now, Lady Harriett was glaring at the man seated across from her. "I suppose you're not fond of cats, either. Not manly enough for you."

"Right you'd be, my lady. They're sneaky creatures, if you ask me."

Lady Harriett continued to glare at the man while refusing to further the conversation.

For her part, Caroline was glad they'd come with Mr. Blythe-Carrington today. Now Lady Harriett had been able to see for herself how unsuitable he was.

"What about mice, Mr. Blythe-Carrington?" Caroline asked, barely able to keep herself from smiling. "Have you ever thought of having one for a pet?"

"Good lord, no!"

"What a pity," Caroline said. "Lady Harriett has the sweetest little mouse for a pet. He has his own house, and she even kisses his fur." Caroline turned to her companion. "Mice do have fur, do they not?"

"Yes. It's very soft. They make adorable pets." Lady Harriett directed her attention across the way to their host. "The sun seems to have ducked behind the clouds. I'm rather cold. Please take us home."

A look of annoyance on his face, he instructed his driver to turn around.

Caroline was relieved Lady Harriett had apparently made the decision on her own that Mr. Blythe-Carrington was not the man for her. She never wanted to be the person who had to warn the lady against fortune hunters. Lady Harriett's prettiness, rank, and endearing personality should be enough to capture most men's hearts, and Caroline felt sure the lady's other suitors were genuinely attracted to her—not to her dowry.

She was also aware that no men of their social circle would ever consider marrying a woman without a dowry. Women like Caroline were doomed to spend their lives as spinsters in service to others.

"Tell me, Mr. Blythe-Carrington," Lady Harriett said, "have you ever considered standing for the House of Commons?"

"Why would I want to do that? It's a vast waste of money. Electioneering is very expensive, and what would I get out of it?"

Lady Harriett could only barely conceal her impatience with the man. "You'd be helping your country."

"I'll leave that to older fellows like your brother. Besides, Devere has pots of money. I'd rather spend mine on horses."

By now, they had left the park and were moving along toward Curzon Street.

Though Caroline knew Lady Harriett had used the excuse of sudden cloudiness in order to rid herself of Blythe-Carrington's obnoxious company, the weather really was turning cooler. She was almost certain that within the hour the heavens would burst with significant rainfall.

Lady Harriett entered her house first, with Caroline just behind her. As soon as Lady Harriett stepped into the marble-floored foyer, she froze. And screamed.

Caroline rushed to her and saw the source of her companion's anguish.

Preening Pumpkin was descending the staircase, her sharp teeth clamped down on something dark, something with a . . . oh, no, a protruding mouse's tail. Caroline, too, froze. She knew she should remove the mouse from the cat's mouth, but she was too skittish to do so. In one way, she was relieved that she wouldn't have to fear the mouse anymore, for he clearly had not survived the cat's attack.

It was so unlike Caroline to have so irrational a fear, but she couldn't help it. More than once, she'd lain in her bed terrified that Mr. Mousie had escaped his *house* and found his way into her bedchamber. She cringed at the thought of him crawling in her bed.

Lady Harriett's eyes tightly shut against the offensive sight, she began to wail.

Caroline finally came to her senses—not bravely enough to remove Mr. Mousie from Pumpkin's deadly grip, but enough to approach the footman.

"You're not the front hall footman."

"I'm filling in for him. He seems to have disappeared."

She nodded. "Forgive me for not knowing your name, sir," she began. The fine-looking fellow in the Devere crimson livery was about the same age as Lady Harriett. Caroline would have no difficulty believing all the housemaids in love with him.

"It's Frederick."

Caroline's voice dropped to a whisper. "Frederick, I hate to ask you, but you look so strong and fearless, I was hoping you could . . . ah, remove the mouse from the cat's mouth and . . . ah, see to it the mouse gets a fitting burial. Lady Harriett's exceedingly fond of the creature."

"I am at your service, miss." He approached the staircase just as Pumpkin reached the bottom step. When Frederick went to lift the cat, the orange cat's paw swiped at him, drawing blood.

Lady Harriett shrieked. "Oh, Pumpkin, you are too, too bad!" Then she tightly shut her eyes again, tears still streaming down her now-reddened face.

Frederick was not to be deterred. He grabbed the big cat, making sure to keep its feet dangling while he forced the lifeless mouse from its mouth before setting down the cat and leaving, disappearing behind a door used only by the servants.

Caroline drew the weeping Lady Harriett into her arms. "I know how difficult it is to lose something you love."

"It's my fault. I should have known what a clever cat Pumpkin is. She would have had no difficulty opening Mr. Mousie's door." Sniff. Sniff.

"Don't blame yourself. What do you know of the life expectancy of a mouse? It could be that their life span is not great. He might not have had much time left. And you mustn't be too harsh on Pumpkin."

"I am vexed with her, but I know she doesn't understand that what she's done is wicked."

The ladies began to mount the stairs, and Lady Harriett appeared to have calmed considerably. One attached to pets learns to accept the inevitability of loss.

When they were halfway up, the front door opened, and Lord Devere greeted them, then his brows lowered. "What's wrong with Harry?"

"My cat ate Mr. Mousie."

If Caroline wasn't mistaken, his lordship had to squelch a smile. "I'm sorry. I know how fond you were of the creature." He handed his hat to the footman and started for the library. "I'll see you ladies at dinner."

They reached Lady Harriett's chambers first. "Would you prefer that I stay with you?" Caroline asked.

"No, I'll be fine. You need to dress for dinner."

"Shall I ask the footman to come remove Mr. Mousie's house, or do you plan to adopt another mouse?"

"I must think on this before I make a rash decision."

Caroline hugged her and continued on to her own bedchamber. She opened the door and screamed.

CHAPTER TEN

SOMEONE HAD DESTROYED her room. The silken bed coverings had been stripped away and thrown on the floor. The Sevres vases upon the mantel now laid on their sides. The drawers on her French writing desk had been flung to the floor, their contents sprayed across the carpet. Even the portrait that hung above the mantel now stood against a wall. The doors of her linen press gaped open, and her clothing heaped on the floor.

Nothing in her chamber remained untouched from the onslaught.

In one agonizing second, she was transported back to that night at Heathergate, the night Mrs. Wyndham had been murdered. Mrs. Wyndham's rooms had been searched in just such a manner.

This could not be a coincidence. Could it? Her heartbeat roared in her chest. Her hands trembled uncontrollably.

Her first fear was that the culprit—possibly the murderer—was still there. Nothing could have persuaded her to set one foot into that room.

She allowed herself to hope hers was not the only room that had been searched. Perhaps it was merely a jewel thief.

But the fact Lady Harriett had not screamed upon entering her chamber revealed that Caroline's room most likely was the only one so scrutinized. Which meant the murderer somehow had tracked her here. He must have been looking for Mrs. Wyndham's journal.

She'd never been more terrified.

Lady Harriett raced from her chamber, and one quick look into Caroline's bedchamber made any questions unnecessary.

Heavy footsteps pounded up the stairs.

And then Lord Devere was there.

Even though she still was not ready to go into her chamber, she no longer felt such imminent peril.

He looked from her through the open door into her room. "What the bloody hell has happened?"

Caroline knew very well what the bloody hell had happened, but she was not at liberty to say. She shrugged and looked at Lady Harriett. "Your room was untouched?"

"Yes." Lady Harriett's brows lowered. "Perhaps the thief mistook your chamber for mine."

Caroline attempted to gather her composure, though it was impossible to keep the quiver from her voice. "That must explain it. I have nothing of value."

"Are you sure?" he asked. "You ought to try to determine if anything's missing."

She shook her head.

"You're afraid to go into the chamber?" he asked.

A nod was her only response. It was difficult to keep her tears from gushing.

His lordship stormed into the room, cursing under his breath. "We'll have the parlor maid put things back to rights for you."

"Yes, and you can get ready for dinner in my chamber." Lady Harriett's gaze went to the crumpled clothing on her companion's floor. "It's best if you wear one of my dresses tonight."

Devere looked under her bed, and when he straightened up, his gaze went to her. "Rest assured, Miss Rutherford, no one is in your chamber. Have no fears about coming in here."

He met them in the corridor. "And I'm going to speak with the servants." Anger sharpened his voice. "How could this happen in daylight with a house full of servants?"

She had a very good idea. One of the servants must have been bought by the man who killed Betsy Wyndham.

WHERE IN THE devil was that bloody footman? Devere wondered. Jonathan's duties kept him in the entry corridor at the front of the house. Always. It was his domain. It was very unlike him to shirk his duties.

Unless . . . was it possible he was the one responsible for what happened in Miss Rutherford's chamber? Had he found something so valuable it was worth leaving his secure employment? But if he were a thief, wouldn't it have been wiser to have gone into Harriett's chamber?

Devere went to the basement. He needed to speak to the butler.

He found Hopkins overseeing a wine delivery. Hopkins refused to allow any other servants to intrude into his administration of the family's wines. The bald-headed butler looked up when his master entered the chamber. Hopkins quickly erased the puzzled look his employer's unprecedented visit here had prompted.

"I beg a word with you," Devere said.

"Of course, my lord." Hopkins left his duties to join the earl, and they moved into the unoccupied corridor.

"Where's Jonathan?"

"He's not watching the front of the house?"

"He's disappeared, and Miss Rutherford's bedchamber has been searched. Her room was left in disarray. We've yet to establish what, if anything, was taken."

Hopkins' eyes widened. "Today?"

"Indeed. Things were normal when the ladies left about three today. They returned moments ago to find the upheaval in the lady's bedchamber. And no sign of Jonathan."

Devere hated to consider that anyone in his household could be responsible for this deed. Most of them had been with him for years, some of them with the family since before his birth. The newer ones, including Jonathan, had come at the recommendation of Miss Fletcher's unimpeachable agency.

"This is appalling!" Hopkins said. "I will conduct a search to find Jonathan."

"I fear we may have misjudged the fellow. He seems to have gone."

"I thought him such a good sort. He's always watched that door like a bird on a nest."

"I share your confidence in him." Devere drew a deep breath. "From now on, all outer doors will be locked at all times, and you are the only one permitted to open them." It really was horrifying to think of a man entering his sister's or Miss Rutherford's chambers.

Devere was accustomed to entrusting everything to do with domestic matters to Hopkins, but this once he felt compelled to question the other servants himself instead of delegating that duty to his butler. "I mean to personally speak to the other servants about this matter."

He went to the kitchens and questioned the cook and scullery maid, neither of whom he'd ever seen before and both of whom were shocked to have the lord and master enter their domain. The cook had a difficult time looking him in the eyes. She lifted the hem of her apron to cover its soiling around her ample midsection. When she finally was induced to speak, she said, "Twern't no outsiders in here today."

The youthful scullery maid nodded.

"Are you agreeing with the cook or refuting her?" Devere asked the girl.

Her prominent chin jutted out a bit further as she frowned. "Don't know what refuting is, yer lordship, but I do be agreeing with Mrs. Morton."

He could tell the girl was so intimidated by him she was nervous. Which made him feel badly. The girl couldn't be more than sixteen. His voice gentled. "Thank you, Miss? What is your name?"

She dropped into a curtsy. "Annabelle."

"Well, good day to you, Annabelle." His gaze shifted to the cook. "Mrs. Morton. By the way, I've given orders that the outer doors stay locked at all times, and only Hopkins is permitted to open them."

Next, he went to the housekeeper, Mrs. Pryor, who was sitting before a desk in her chambers, the door open. She had served as the Devere housekeeper since he was a lad. Why had he not noticed her hair had gone almost completely gray? He still thought of her as a brunette. As he explained the occurrence that necessitated his visit, her mouth gaped open, her brows lowered.

"I can't believe Jonathan's responsible for this. He's always been such a good lad. I don't know how this could have occurred in broad daylight!" she exclaimed. "I am happy to learn we'll be keeping all the doors locked. I tremble for poor Lady Harriett."

As did he. And for Caroline, too.

"I'll have the upstairs parlor maid restore Miss Rutherford's bedchamber," she said, "and I'll speak to all the maids."

As he went to his bedchamber to prepare for dinner, Hopkins said he could not find Jonathan but, curiously, nothing was missing from the footman's bedchamber.

"That doesn't make sense," Devere said, continuing on to his own bedchamber. The only thing that made any sense was that Jonathan must have mistaken Miss Rutherford's room for Harriett's. What had kept him from advancing to Harriett's room when he found nothing of value in Miss Rutherford's chamber? Perhaps his fear of discovery accounted for his dismissal of other rooms. But why had he not taken his own things when he left?

Devere could not shake loose the bone-deep feeling that something else was at play here. Something that concerned the enigmatic Miss Rutherford.

CONTRIBUTING TO THE dinner conversation was almost impossible for Caroline. She had not recovered from the horrifying discovery that someone had been in her room. A possible murderer.

She'd taken so many precautions to bury Charlotte Robinson, even giving up the name she had answered to for a quarter of a century. How was it possible she had been traced to Devere House in Mayfair? Only one person in this city knew who she really was, and she had full confidence that Miss Fletcher would not have revealed the truth to anyone.

Her only source of relief was that the intruder had not disturbed Lady Harriett's chambers. If Caroline thought her presence would endanger the Beresford family, she would be forced to leave Devere House.

Then, like a building collapsing on top of her, she realized she *would* have to leave. Mrs. Wyndham's killer knew where to find her.

She needed to find a new place to live.

But how could she ever be at liberty to even find a new place to live when she was being watched? The killer would be waiting to find her alone, unprotected. Then he would pounce, like a lion on a mouse.

Leaving Devere House would be the latest in a series of crippling blows that had tormented her these past two years.

Her thoughts kept returning to Devere's anger when he saw what had occurred in his home. She was surprised over the venom in his voice as they had stood there in the corridor outside her open bedchamber door.

He had every right to be angry. For all he knew, his sister's well-being was in jeopardy.

"Rest assured, Miss Rutherford, you will be safe in this house," Lord Devere said. "Henceforth, our doors are to remain locked at all times. I have some troubling news. We believe Jonathan is the one who searched your chambers."

Lady Harriett shook her head adamantly. "No, he wouldn't do that."

"I would have thought the same," Lord Devere said, "but he's disappeared."

"I refuse to believe him capable of such a thing," Lady Harriett insisted.

"I know." Lord Devere frowned. "And the peculiar thing is he took none of his possessions when he left."

Caroline could understand none of it. The search of her chamber, she felt sure, had been orchestrated by the killer of Mrs. Wyndham, and Johnathan could not be associated with that evil man since he'd been here for a few years. Unless . . . he was bribed. That had to explain it. Some people would do anything for money.

"After dinner we ought to go to your chamber so you can determine if anything was stolen," Lady Harriett said.

"If you like, I could come, too," Lord Devere said. "I could tell you were frightened to go into the room earlier."

"I shouldn't wish to inconvenience you, my lord."

Those penetrating dark eyes of his met hers. "You're never an inconvenience, Miss Rutherford."

Lady Harriett cleared her throat and sat up a bit taller, her gaze swinging from Caroline to her brother. "I read in this morning's paper about Alex Muir's speech in the House of Commons yesterday, the impassioned plea against slavery."

His eyebrows raised, Lord Devere looked at his sister as if she had just spouted a gross falsehood. "Since when did my sister read about the occurrences in our government?"

"Your sister's been reading the papers every morning—and not just the gossip tidbits."

He looked at Lady Harriett. "Papers? Plural?"

She nodded, looking as proud as a princess. "I don't just read about you Whigs. I wish to become more informed about all matters of government."

He turned to Caroline. "Is this your doing?"

"I wish I could take credit for it, but I cannot."

"What's responsible for this transformation?" he asked his sister.

"I wish to educate myself about government. It started, I think, when I thought I might be . . . compatible with Mr. Stone. Alex says he's got a bright future in Parliament. But even after I decided that Mr. Stone and I wouldn't suit, I found myself wanting to know about what you and Alex are doing in your respective houses."

"Your sister's been maturing before my very eyes," Caroline said.

"I will own, I'm most pleasantly surprised over your new interest, Harry. Tell me, what are your opinions on slavery?"

"It's not my opinions that matter. You're the one who votes. Will you continue to be opposed to all forms of slavery?"

"I've never hidden the fact I'm strongly opposed to slavery of any kind."

Lady Harriett bestowed a brilliant smile upon her brother. "That's exactly what I was hoping you would say."

"Perhaps the next time I engage in one of those political dinners at the Hollands', both of you ladies could accompany me."

"I should adore that," his sister said.

After dinner, they did go to Caroline's bedchamber. The maid was finishing up. Caroline's trepidation made her feel like a complete ninny, but she could not deny that re-entering that chamber accompanied by his lordship allayed her fears. Even knowing that the culprit was no longer there, she could not shed the fear that spiked through her at the very notion of re-entering the room that so evil a person had defiled.

She had said she possessed nothing of value, but that wasn't entirely true. She did own a string of pearls that had belonged to her mother. After the fire, her only consolation was that she'd taken Mama's pearls on that London visit, the visit that spared her life. Had she not been in London when fire destroyed Babbley, she would have perished along with her father and brother.

She went straight to the drawers of the dressing table. The first one she opened contained her brush and comb. That is where she had stored Mama's pearls. For a brief second, even though she mourned the loss of the heirloom pearls, she almost rejoiced that the intruder just may have been a thief, a thief mistaking her chamber for Lady Harriett's.

Then it occurred to her the maid restoring order to her room would not have known in which drawer Caroline kept the pearls. Drawing in a deep breath, Caroline opened the drawer on the opposite side of the dressing table. And there lay the velvet case which held the pearls. She opened it. And the coiled pearls nestled on a bed of ivory satin.

Now it was confirmed. Whoever had searched her room today—and evidence was pointing to that being Jonathan—had been searching for Mrs. Wyndham's journal.

Her killer would now know Caroline's every move.

She had to escape.

The maid curtseyed and left the chamber. A moment later, her piercing scream rang out from the corridor.

They rushed to her. The hysterical woman stood in front of the linen closet.

Lord Devere went to see the source of her terror. One glance into the closet, and his lordship winced before dropping to the ground.

Caroline hurried to him. He knelt beside Jonathan's body. He turned around. "He's dead."

CHAPTER ELEVEN

NOW CAROLINE HAD two horrific scenes that could never be effaced from her memory. Mrs. Wyndham's lifeless body and the young footman's. She had no doubt the two deaths were connected.

But as upset as she had been over Mrs. Wyndham's death and how it subsequently altered the very course of her life, she was affected even more profoundly by poor Jonathan's because she was responsible for his murder. Had she never come to Devere House, he would still be alive. Her heart wept for the loss of the youthful man.

Later, after Hopkins had overseen the removal of the footman's body, Lord Devere entered his candlelit library, the chamber where he'd sent the ladies to wait while all the unpleasantness was occurring. Lady Harriett had only just stopped sobbing.

A grave expression on his face, he came and joined them on the sofa. "I feel beastly for suspecting Jonathan of searching Miss Rutherford's chamber."

"I told you he couldn't possibly have done it." A fresh bout of sobs commenced from Lady Harriett.

Looking distressed himself, her brother scooted closer and drew her into his arms, patting her reassuringly.

"I know," he murmured soothingly. "We did find a large sum

of money in his chamber, though."

"So you believe someone else paid him to allow entry into the house and search . . . what he thought was Lady Harriett's chamber?" Caroline knew the man who killed Mrs. Wyndham wasn't interested in Lady Harriett's chamber, but she wanted to deflect suspicion from herself. "And the other person then slayed Jonathan because he could identify him?"

Lord Devere nodded. "How clever you are, Miss Rutherford. I keep wondering why your chamber and not Harry's."

Caroline shrugged. "Jonathan must have gotten mixed up. After all, his duties rarely took him beyond what's commonly called the porter's hall."

Lady Harriett shook her head. "That can't be. Jonathan often carried packages to my chambers."

Lord Devere's gaze met Caroline's. "Perhaps Miss Rutherford is in possession of something more valuable than jewels?"

Her heartbeat roared. He was far too close to the mark. It was imperative she make him believe Lady Harriett's chamber was the true target, though she hated herself for perpetuating more lies. Her eyes never leaving his, she shrugged. "How can the daughter of a country clergyman possess something of significant value?" At least she hadn't told an outright lie.

One last sniff, and Lady Harriett straightened and faced her. "Was your mother, per chance, from an aristocratic family?"

"No," Caroline answered.

"You ladies go on to bed. I have much to consider." Lord Devere stood. "I'll walk you to your chambers. I know Miss Rutherford may still be frightened to enter her room."

Because Lord Devere had come to her chamber and because she was aware all the doors were locked, when Caroline lay in her bed that night, she knew that, for now, she was safe from the killer's grasp. But what about tomorrow? Or any time she left Devere House? She felt certain her life was in danger.

The only answer to her perilous dilemma was to flee. But how could she do that when she was being watched? And even if she managed to devise a successful method of escape, where would she live? How would she get by with almost no money? She wasn't due to get paid until the quarter.

Even the contemplation of having to leave Devere House was as grievous as the loss of a loved one. After the unspeakable losses she had already endured these past two years, how was she to survive this? Leaving here would be one of the hardest things she'd ever had to do.

Never again would she find so desirable a position. Calling her employment desirable was an understatement. It was the *perfect* situation. She had lovely accommodations. She was permitted to eat at the family dining table and treated almost as a member of their family. The lady to whom she served as companion could not have been more pleasant. Caroline received a lovely wardrobe and mingled with the upper classes, even though she would never be one of their ilk, a reality she fully accepted.

Most of all . . . if she left Devere House, she would never again be kissed by the Earl of Devere. She knew she would go to her grave without finding another man who was his equal.

But what man could be his equal? She'd seen enough of the *ton* by now to know that among the kingdom's most sought-after bachelors, none could compare to her Lord Devere. This earl possessed any attribute a woman could desire in a man—rank, wealth, good looks, intelligence, leadership, and congeniality.

And poor, plain inconsequential Caroline Rutherford had done the unthinkable. She had fallen in love with the unobtainable peer.

Even worse, now she was going to have to leave and never allow herself to see him again.

Sleep was impossible. She kept trying to devise a plan of

escape. Her first thought was of donning her black mourning gown and stealing away in the wee hours of the morning. But what if the killer was rich enough to post men watching her around the clock? It was very likely. Mrs. Wyndham's lavish lifestyle had been funded by wealthy men.

Nothing could be more perilous than a lone prey confronting her would-be slayer on dark, deserted streets. Almost on a daily basis, she read about murders that occurred nightly in London.

During those sleepless hours, she continued thinking of scenarios ranging from slipping out the back door at shops frequented by Lady Harriett to getting "lost" in a large crowd. None satisfied.

She gave considerable consideration to feigning an illness that would send her to bed until such time as she could implement her plan. That would not be fair to Lady Harriett. Her Season was so short, Caroline hated to deprive the girl of any of those activities she so thoroughly enjoyed. Caroline knew full well his lordship was depending upon her to see to it that his sister made the good match she deserved, and Caroline hated to disappoint either of them.

Just before daybreak, she hit on a plan. It might take some time to iron out the details, but she felt fairly certain she could bribe one of the house maids—the one whose hair and size were much like her own average looks—to switch clothes with her. Dressed as the maid, Caroline could leave by way of the servants' back door during broad daylight and vanish into the city.

There was one problem she would have to solve first. His lordship had given orders that no one could open the locked exterior doors except Hopkins, and the butler would know she wasn't the maid.

She also made some decisions about how she would go about trying to protect herself until she was able to escape. If she had her way, she would never leave the house without Lord Devere. No man would dare accost him.

But, alas, she had not the power to dictate to her powerful

employer.

She would continue accompanying Lady Harriett to all her functions, but how could two slender young women protect themselves against the evil forces at work here?

Then she got an idea.

THE SILKEN DRAPERIES in his bedchamber had been yanked open, flooding his room with far more light than Devere wished. He'd paced his library until dawn, pondering the danger that threatened his household. And drinking too much brandy.

He planted his elbows on the bed and raised himself to glare at his man. "Pray, Dryer, why do you awaken me at so ungodly an hour in the morning?"

"It's no longer morning, my lord. Miss Rutherford's been waiting nearly two hours to have a word with you."

He bolted from the bed. "Well, man, hurry up! Make me presentable to the lady." It was unlike Miss Rutherford to initiate a conversation. Was everything all right with Harriett?

Fifteen minutes later, he met his sister's companion in his sunny library. Her clean and recently ironed sprigged muslin dress was as fresh-looking as she. The lack of artifice in her face made her seem much closer to Harriett's age than to her own. Had he noticed before the light sprinkle of freckles on her nose? Perhaps they were responsible for her youthful appearance. "You needed to speak to me?"

She stood by his desk and nodded. It reminded him of the day they'd met. He'd sat behind the desk then. It seemed so long ago.

"Please, Miss Rutherford, take a seat wherever you like."

She went to sit in one of a pair of comfortable arm chairs in front of the tall window. She couldn't possibly have known it, but on sun-filled days like this, the spot she chose was his favorite in the house.

He sat in the other chair, facing her. "How can be of help to you?" he asked.

"I've been thinking about yesterday's horrifying occurrences."

A rumble in his gut, he prayed she wasn't going to give her notice.

"Since the intruder took nothing, I fear for your sister's safety. He had to have mistaken my room for hers. My biggest fear is that he may stalk Lady Harriett."

He had heard of men whose deranged minds had them steal women's undergarments. Is that what had motivated yesterday's actions? His stomach churned with disgust.

In other ways, Miss Rutherford's statement also stunned him. First, it should have been he, and not his employee, who showed such concern for his sister's well-being. The very thought of a man stalking or harming Harry terrified him. Secondly, he was shocked that Miss Rutherford had just spoken several sentences at once to him. That was a first. "Have you any suggestions as to how I can address this potential peril?"

"I do. Might I suggest that whenever we leave Devere House, you assign a footman to accompany us?"

It was a very good plan. His footmen were strapping fellows. And he could see to it that they be armed with swords though he doubted any of them had been trained in fencing. As he had.

As he pondered it, he realized there was no need to send footmen. It was his duty to protect Harry.

And Caroline Rutherford.

"I'm in favor of your plan. With one variation."

Her fine pale brown eyebrows elevated.

"I shall accompany you ladies."

She was struck silent for a moment. "I would never have so imposed on your lordship's valuable time."

He knew she referred to his parliamentary duties. He knew this because he had come to know of this woman's consuming interest in all things political. "Are you afraid I'll miss the vote to abolish slavery?" he asked, a mischievous smile on his face.

"It could do irreparable harm if you are absent from the House of Lords."

"Are you saying every Whig vote is needed?"

"Yes."

"A girl after my own heart." *Good lord, what have I just said?* "However, Miss Rutherford, I've been involved in parliamentary matters long enough to know when it's necessary for me to be present for an important vote. I will not shirk my responsibilities."

"Forgive me for insinuating otherwise." She bit at her lip as if she were debating whether she should continue. "I know how conscientious you are, my lord, how noble."

Was she referring to his nobility of character—that morality that kept him from actually seducing the woman—no matter how much he longed to? "As to the matter at hand, for the time being, count on me escorting the pair of you wherever you go."

"I dare say it's merely a temporary solution. If only there were a way we could identify the culprit."

Her tongue was loosening. Not a great deal, but a definite improvement. "Would that we could identify him, but I am clueless as to how we can."

"As am I."

He leaned back in his chair. "So what does my sister have planned for today?"

"As it's not the day for callers, she had hoped to ride in Hyde Park." Her glance went to the window where open draperies revealed a perfect summer day for a drive in the park. He'd not allowed himself such a purposeless pleasure in years.

"And what is my sister doing now?"

"She's still serious about reading her morning newspapers."

"This is, indeed, a complete departure for my sister. Does she truly read the parliamentary accounts?"

"That seems to have become her impetus in reading the papers."

"I cannot believe that you're not to be credited for the sudden change in my sister."

"If you must credit someone, credit yourself. You've set a good example."

"I'm jolly well pleased with the changes. In fact, I'm very proud of Harriett's recent maturation."

"Being in Society has enabled her to transition from girl to young woman. You have every right to be proud of her. She's making many sage choices."

He still believed Miss Rutherford deserved some of the credit for his sister's newfound wisdom.

Hopkins tapped at the door, and then he entered. "A most unusual delivery has just been made, my lord, and I wished to check with you to see that it is something that meets with your lordship's approval."

"What, pray tell, is it?" Devere asked.

Hopkins cleared his throat. "It's a rather large cage which appears to contain two gray birds."

A smile broke across his face as Devere leapt to his feet. "The doves!" His gaze met Caroline Rutherford's.

She smiled, too. "For Lady Harriett?"

"Yes. It's my surprise. I wanted to take her mind off Mr. Mousie's loss."

"What a sweet brother you are. She will love them."

CAROLINE HAD BEEN right. In the weeks since she'd arrived at Devere House, she had never seen Lady Harriett so happy as when Lord Devere strode into the lady's study and set the towering birdcage on a table.

"Love birds! For me!" She raced across her study and threw her arms around her brother. "You are the best of brothers."

Then she sped to the cage to look at the two wide-bodied, gray birds. "Are they male and female?"

"That's what I requested."

Caroline crossed the chamber and peered at the cage. "How does one tell the difference?" As soon as she said it, she regretted her words. If there were a dangling male protrusion—which she did not believe birds possessed—she would rather not hear about it in front of his lordship.

"One can't just by looking," Lady Harriett said. "The proof comes after a period of time passes."

"How?" Caroline asked.

"The females always lay two eggs. If, after a period of time, there are no eggs, you know you've gotten two males." Lady Harriett said.

"And if you've got four eggs, you've got two females," Caroline said with a laugh.

"I don't believe two females could mate." Lord Devere moved closer.

Caroline looked up at him. Just hearing the word *mate* on his lips physically stirred her in a way she'd never before experienced.

"Doves mate for life." His dark eyes held hers.

She was powerless to break the connection. "Yes, I've heard."

"I cannot wait until they mate," Lady Harriett exclaimed.

Still, Caroline and Lord Devere gazed into each other's eyes while he addressed his sister. "You will have to provide them with nesting bowls and perhaps some twigs and such with which to build a nest. After . . ."

After they mate. Color crept into Caroline's cheeks, and she turned back to look at the birds.

It was probably for the best that she leave Devere House. Nothing could ever have come from her love of this man, and the longer she was with him, the more dangerous it was for her heart.

"THE JOURNAL HAD to be in that chamber!" he said.

"We looked everywhere—even behind the portrait that hung over her fireplace," Johnson defended.

"Then you weren't in the right room," their employer said, fuming.

"But we were. As soon as the ladies left the house, the footman we bribed let us in the front door and marched us up the stairs himself to the lady's room."

Goddard nodded. "And the footman stood watch to make sure we weren't discovered."

Their employer, his face blanched with anger, got up and began to pace his book-lined library. "I rescind my order about killing her. I need the woman alive. She's the only one who knows where that journal is, and it's imperative that it gets into my possession."

Even as he spoke, he wondered why she had not tried to contact him, not tried to extract money from him. Like Betsy had done. What was she waiting for? She would have to know about his vast wealth.

He spun around to face the two miscreants. "Had you been discovered upstairs in Lord Devere's house, how were you going to explain your presence there?"

"The footman was going to say we was inspectors from the tax office." Johnson coughed. "His services didn't come cheap. Said he had a good position there and couldn't take the chance of getting sacked unless he received a large amount of money."

"How much?"

"Fifty quid. And now he'll not be able to spend a penny of it."

"Why?"

"We couldn't leave any witnesses."

He closed his eyes and gritted his teeth. "You didn't kill him?"

Both men nodded.

"We thought you'd be pleased," Johnson said. "I was gonna take back the fifty quid, but it wasn't on him."

"You fools! Now it will be even harder to get at Charlotte

Robinson. Or Caroline Rutherford, as she now calls herself." He did wish they'd gotten back the fifty quid. It was more than a year's salary to a man in the footman's position. He went to his desk, unlocked the drawer, and counted out coins before offering them to his lackeys. "You did restore the woman's chamber before you left?"

Both men frowned. "You didn't say nothing about putting things back to rights."

"You morons! Now she'll know that I know her whereabouts. It won't be easy to abduct her."

Johnson stepped forward. "Don't you worry none. We'll abduct her."

"I want one of you to have eyes on that house day and night. When you see her alone, you'll know what to do. But remember, you're not to kill her until we get the journal."

CHAPTER TWELVE

IN THE WEEKS Caroline had lived at Devere House, his lordship had never summoned her to his library. Until today. Though she didn't think she had done anything to incur his displeasure, she was, nevertheless, nervous. Why did he wish to speak to her? Had she done something she wasn't supposed to do?

Her stomach dropped, and her heartbeat raced. What if he'd discovered she'd being lying to him about who she really was? Had he learned the truth? He must know she was responsible for Jonathan's murder.

Clutching her knitted shawl about her shoulders for warmth, she entered his library. It was a dreary, rainy day, with the ensuing coolness necessitating a fire. She'd expected to see him seated behind his desk, the position he frequently occupied, but today, he was seated on the sofa before the fire. The room had never been more comforting.

He stood when she entered. "Please, Miss Rutherford, come sit on the sofa."

His friendly tone allayed her nervousness. She wasn't being sent to the woodshed after all. She came to sit on the opposite end of the velvet sofa from him.

"I'm thankful you ordered fires today, my lord," she said as an icebreaker, offering him a smile.

"Even though it's summer, these rainy English summer days

can be awfully cold."

"Indeed." She looked down at the folded hands in her lap.

"I wanted to seek your opinion on my sister's prospects. I expect she confides in you, as I believe the two of you have become quite close. None of my sisters have ever been as mad to marry as Harriett so, quite naturally, I worry she'll rush into marriage with one not quite suitable."

"I had the same fear when I first came here. She was so eager to wed. But she's proven to be more discerning than we gave her credit for."

"I am gratified that our drawing room is filled with her admirers each day she's home to receive callers."

"She's highly sought after, to be sure."

"Is there any one man in particular whom she appears to favor?"

"I don't believe so. I have noticed that when she first meets a man she considers to be highly eligible, she ever so briefly fancies herself in love, but upon becoming more familiar with the suitor, her mind changes. The knight's armor appears to chink upon further acquaintance." Caroline gave a little laugh. "Whether she admits it or not, she's very much as discerning as her elder sisters were."

Now, he chuckled. "And they both married very well. Moreover, each of my brothers-in-law have earned wide respect for being such admirable men."

"I believe Lady Harriett will also make a fine selection."

"I am relieved more than I can say. It's no bad thing to take after Sophia and Maryann—or Mary as she now prefers to be known."

"I agree."

"And she's curbing her propensity to blurt out silly, girlish statements?"

Caroline hesitated a moment before responding. "Only once or twice have I had to employ a forehead swipe."

"Oh, yes, your ingenious brow swipe," he said with a smile

and a twinkling in his dark eyes.

Whenever he smiled at her like that, she experienced the same effervescence as that produced by champagne.

He cleared his throat. "The other matter I wished to speak to you about concerns that unpleasantness that occurred in your chamber and resulted in Jonathan's death." His pensive gaze held hers. "Understandably, such an occurrence is very upsetting. I . . . we don't want to lose you, Caroline."

He'd called her by her Christian name again. Her heartbeat roared, and she was certain she was trembling. Knowing that she was responsible for Jonathan's death, she felt like a traitor.

"I vow," he continued, "I will protect you."

She kept thinking about his statement *I don't want to lose you.* Yet she knew that, because of that reprehensible act, she could not stay. She didn't know how to respond. Even though her very existence here was founded on a series of lies, she could not add one more lie by telling him she would not leave.

Finally, she broke her silence. "I know you will do everything in your power to protect me. And Lady Harriett, of course." Guilt coursed through her. Because of her, he was being forced to alter his schedules and dance attendance on a pair of young women. It was an untenable situation.

The only solution was for her to go away. Once she devised a scheme to leave Devere House, she would write his lordship a letter explaining her lies. He deserved to know that it was she, and not his sister, who had been the target of an evil man's quest.

"It looks as if the rain will keep us from a ride in the park today," he said.

"Yes. I thought Lady Harriett would be disappointed, but she says it will give her an opportunity to catch up on her correspondence. She's madly writing away."

"You have letters to write?"

If only there were someone to whom she could write. She had not a soul in the world. Even though Charlotte Robinson no longer had a family, she did have a handful of friends in London, but Charlotte was now buried, and Caroline had no one.

Caroline supposedly was one of a large brood and should probably act as if she had siblings, but she could hardly post to nonexistent people since all the posts from Devere House had to be franked by his lordship.

"I am ashamed to say I'm a very poor correspondent," she said.

"That pleases me."

She gave him a puzzled look.

"I was hoping to persuade you to play chess with me."

"I dare say I'm an even poorer chess player than a correspondent."

"I doubt that my impression of you as being always competent is wrong."

"I am flattered by your confidence, my lord."

"Then will you permit me to set up the chess board?"

As low as she felt, she found herself laughing at the absurdity of his comment. "It is not I who command *you*. I am at your command."

WHILE HE POSITIONED the chess pieces on the board, he kept thinking of her simple statement. *I am at your command.* The very notion that this alluring woman could be subservient to his needs aroused him.

They then faced each other across the small game table. It was an intimate setting. The library, with its walnut paneled walls, plush velvets, and comforting fire, had always been his favorite chamber in the house, especially on one of those rainy, gray days that made venturing out of doors an unwelcome prospect.

Caroline Rutherford's presence here in this favored room completed his satisfaction. There was nowhere else he would rather be than in this chamber with this intoxicating woman at this moment in time. He could neither explain nor deny his attraction to her. It was just there, one of those indisputable facts like the color of his eyes.

The game's initial moves required no concentration on either of their parts—which was good, considering he couldn't get his mind off her. Her soft rose scent wafted across to him, adding to the ways in which this proper young woman invaded his mind with improper thoughts.

What was there about her that affected him so profoundly? His simmering gaze went from her fair face to the same pale skin that dipped enticingly into the bodice of her pink gown. With every rise and fall of her breasts, he fought his attraction. He longed to touch her, to slip the dress off those ivory shoulders, to caress those breasts, to kiss them, to kiss her until she begged to become his.

His gaze skipped to watch as she moved her pawn with delicate fingers. Her elegance contributed to her appeal. The way she sat, the way she spoke softly with little inflection, everything about her quietly proclaimed the woman's restrained grace.

As the play progressed, he also realized her claims of ineptitude in chess were actually just more evidence of her modesty. She did not play like a novice.

They were not so intent on their game that they neglected to converse. To his surprise, she initiated the conversation. "I read in the paper about Madame de Staël's visit to Holland House."

"I'm sorry we didn't get to go. What was it Harry had you doing that night?"

"A ball at Lady Jersey's."

He gave her a look of mock displeasure. "Last I heard, Berkeley Square mansion was also Lord Jersey's."

"I stand deservedly corrected. It's just that her ladyship's personality is so much the dominant one."

"I agree."

"I suppose one in possession of such vast wealth as that inher-

CHERYL BOLEN

ited by Lady Jersey accounts for one's consequence, also."

"I, for one, do not ascribe to such a practice," he said. "My admiration is far greater for those noted for their accomplishments rather than their wealth."

She peered up at him with those wide, mossy eyes. "Is that why you work so hard in the House of Lords?"

He shrugged. "I did not want to be known as that young man who inherited the Beresford family fortune."

"You wanted to be remembered for what you did for your country and your countrymen."

"That is a guiding goal of mine, one I've not yet achieved."

"You've achieved much."

"But there's much more work to be done."

"You will certainly get no argument from me. What will you be channeling your efforts into next?"

"Equality of representation must be addressed. Look at Birmingham. A huge population with not a single Member of Parliament representing them."

She smiled. "You must be a proponent of the system in place in America."

"It's remarkable that such a young nation has superseded anything accomplished by its mother country."

"Theirs is a flawless system of government, in my opinion," she said. "It was time for a substantial change. Monarchies, by their very nature, do not represent people."

"And our history is rife with megalomanic monarchs who did nothing for the people and everything for themselves."

"It's good that our kings now must bow to Parliament."

He sighed. "I will own, I'm no fan of our spendthrift regent, but it wouldn't be Britain if we had no Royal Family. I am a proponent of tradition."

"You sound like my father." Her mouth clamped shut, then she added, "Of course, men of the cloth are traditionalists by nature, do you not agree?"

He chuckled. "More so in the Roman church than in ours."

"Yes, it is much older than ours."

"Your father must have been a well-informed and well-read man."

"He was," she said solemnly.

"I suppose he tutored boys before they went off to university."

She did not respond for a moment. "He did. One with as many mouths to feed as my father had to increase his income any way he could."

"It's my good fortune he could provide no dowry for you. Otherwise you'd never have come to Devere House. Your hand in marriage would have been eagerly sought."

She quickly looked away from his sultry gaze. "That's kind of you to say, my lord, though I doubt the veracity of your words."

His hand covered hers. "You're a very desirable woman, Caroline."

She pulled her hand away and stood. "Perhaps we can finish the game later." Then, without looking at him, she turned and left.

He felt like a fool. He'd gone and spoiled the pleasant afternoon because he bloody well couldn't control himself.

HOW COULD SUCH a pleasant afternoon have caused her such distress, Caroline wondered as she paced her chamber. It had been enjoyable and painful.

Being so close to Lord Devere in that comforting library was her happiest occurrence in several years. When they'd first faced each other across the chess table, she'd been suffused with a blossoming sense of complete well-being. For those few moments, she allowed herself to forget the sinister forces that threatened her. For those moments, there was no one else in her universe except Lord Devere and her.

Then she'd mistakenly brought up the subject of her father. Her real father. The Honorable Matthew Robinson, a well-respected Whig who had served a distinguished career in the House of Commons. Why would her fictional father, the country clergyman, have so acute an interest in governmental affairs?

She hoped Lord Devere had not detected her distress and quick recovery when she shifted to talk of a country parson. And when he'd brought up the topic of her father's tutoring, she'd immediately thought of her brother, Mark, who'd been tutored by the village vicar before he went off to Oxford. Thinking of her father and brother had made her morose.

When his lordship touched her and spoke about her desirability, it was more than she could bear. Nothing could ever come of her love of him, especially now that she had to leave.

CHAPTER THIRTEEN

"WHERE HAS MY brother gone?" Lady Harriett asked Hopkins. Caroline had followed her down the stairs to Lord Devere's library.

"He was called away to the House of Lords."

Lady Harriett stomped her foot. "But I had plans. Miss Rutherford and I were to hear Mr. Bentham speak."

It pleased Caroline that her companion had developed an interest in progressive political philosophy. She was just as eager to hear Jeremy Bentham speak as Lady Harriett was.

"His lordship said he hoped not to be too late," Hopkins said.

The young lady's eyes narrowed with disdain. "We'll not miss this opportunity. Mr. Bentham is getting along in years. This might be our only chance to hear the great man speak." Eyeing the butler, she said, "Please have the coach sent around."

"But, my lady, your brother said you're not to leave the house without him," Hopkins protested.

Caroline set a gentle hand on the lady's arm. "We should wait for Lord Devere."

Lady Harriett's voice hardened. "You can wait for him, but I'm not!"

The idea of leaving Devere House without his lordship's protection terrified Caroline, but she would be shirking her duties if she allowed Lady Harriett to go by herself.

Hopkins cleared his throat. "I will at least send Frederick with you."

Minutes later, the ladies sat on the coach's forward-facing seat as it turned onto Piccadilly. Caroline peered from the coach's window to see if they were being followed. It was difficult to tell because the street was so snarled with a variety of conveyances. The congestion gave Caroline a sense of security.

Which proved to be false.

Right in the midst of stalled traffic, their carriage door was ripped open and a scruffy man yanked Caroline from her seat while a second man—equally as unkempt and ill-dressed— muffled her cries by tying a cloth around her mouth. Harriett screamed. Caroline kicked and tried with all her might to break free but was unable to do so.

Before the Devere coachman or Frederick had the opportunity to get down off the box, Caroline was hurled onto the back of a dray, which had pulled alongside their coach. One of the men held her down while the other bound her hands and feet with rope. Then a tarp was thrown over her as the coach quickly turned off the busy street. One man stayed beside her to prevent her from leaping from the vehicle as it turned sharply and sped away from Piccadilly.

Her ankles and wrists stung from the rope cutting into them, and she was in total darkness. The sound of Lady Harriett's screams grew more dim as the dray raced away. She knew not which direction it was headed. But she had a good idea these men would kill her just as they'd killed poor Jonathan.

NOT LONG AFTER he'd arrived at the White Chamber at the Palace of Westminster, a page from his house came barreling into the chamber, so out of breath he could barely speak. "Mr. Hopkins sent this." He handed Devere a note that read: *Your sister and Miss*

Rutherford disobeyed your orders not to leave the house.

Devere cursed. Where in the devil were they planning on going? He had counted on Miss Rutherford to keep up with those matters for him, and he especially counted on her to rein in his impetuous sister, who was far too accustomed to getting her own way. He was most vexed with both ladies. He had hoped Miss Rutherford would have been able to exert more control over his willful sister.

Grumbling, he left the chamber. It was unlikely that any problem would arise from him not being there to offer protection to the ladies but, even so, his sister must be shown that she should not disobey his orders. No matter where she was, he planned to embarrass her by forcing her to come home.

Since no rain clouds marred the skies, he'd chosen to ride his saddle horse that day—an example set by his father, who for years while serving in the House of Lords cursed the traffic in London. Riding a horse made weaving in and out of snarled conveyances much easier and significantly reduced his commute time.

As soon as he entered his house, he heard his sister's hysterical cries. Something was wrong. His heart pounding, he raced upstairs to the drawing room. It wrung his heart to see Harriett so disconsolate while at the same time he was relieved to see that she appeared unharmed. "What's the matter?"

Anguish twisted her reddened, tear-slickened face. "The most horrible thing! It's Miss Rutherford!"

A knife slashing into his heart could not have been more painful. Miss Rutherford had been killed. He should never have left them. He should have known, because of her mysterious ways, the man who killed Jonathan had his sights on Caroline, not Harriett.

He could only barely eke out the words. "What happened?" He moved to his distraught sister.

"As soon as our coach got to Piccadilly, two horrid men opened the door and snatched her. They bound her mouth and, as quick as a flash, tied her hands and feet and took off in a dray.

Our coachman could not follow because he was cut off by other conveyances." She sniffed.

As dreadful as this intelligence was, he nearly collapsed in relief. *She's not dead.*

"I tried to leap after her, but one of those odious men slammed the coach door on me." She held up her hand that was sheathed in a blood-stained glove.

Fury bolted through him. "Let me see that! Your hand could be broken."

She shook her head. "It's not broken. It just hurts like the devil."

"Killing's too good for those beasts."

She drew a long breath. "There's one slim kernel of hope."

His brows rose. Dare he hope?

"Billy, bless the dear child, did run off after the dray, but I have little hope of him being able to catch them." Her shoulders heaved from her sobs. "It's all my fault. She asked me to stay, but I refused. If anything happens to Miss Rutherford, I shall throw myself from the top of St. Paul's."

If anything happens. Like death. It was too horrendous to contemplate. "You couldn't have known that evil men had designs on Miss Rutherford."

But he should have. He had known there was a strong likelihood she wasn't who she said she was.

His words had no effect upon her. The sobbing continued. He drew her into his arms. "We'll find her."

He had little confidence in his own words.

She sniffed. "I should be severely punished."

"What you're experiencing now is ample punishment." He drew away from her, produced a handkerchief, and dabbed at her slick cheeks before presenting the handkerchief to her.

"Thank you," she uttered.

"I've got to find her."

"But how?"

"Would that I knew. Perhaps a Bow Street Runner." *If it's not too late.* "Tell me everything you remember about the men who abducted her."

She daintily blew her nose. "The one who yanked her from her seat was not a young man. Probably fifty. Grayish whiskers and shaggy gray, leathery skin, as if he spent much time in the outdoors. His clothing was shabby, and his voice was most definitely that of one from the lower classes. The other man was a bit younger but also poorly groomed and dressed. I didn't hear that one speak."

"And how would you describe the dray?"

She shrugged. "Typical."

"Drawn by one horse or two?"

She thought for a moment. "I remember! Two horses."

"What color?"

"Black."

He heard voices coming from the ground floor. One of them sounded like a boy's. Their tiger, Billy. Excited, yet afraid of what the lad could tell them, Devere hurried downstairs. "Do you know where she is, Billy?" he blurted out as soon as he reached the bottom step.

"Indeed I do, my lord."

Devere could Hallelujah! the heavens. "Can you show me?"

The lad nodded.

"Hopkins! Have three horses brought around immediately. Frederick, you're to come with us." Riding horses was the quickest way to get about in the Capital. He strapped on a sword, shoved a knife in his boot, and got his pistol and powder. Soon, he, the footman, and the slender boy had mounted their respective horses and were heading toward The City.

He was impressed that one as young and inexperienced as Billy could find his way around London so well. He must be blessed with an uncommon sense of direction. Thank God. "Tell me, Billy, did you run all the way to The City after those terrible men?"

"I did, my lord. I feared they were going to kill the nice lady, but I peeked in the building where they're keeping her, and they haven't killed her yet. They keep asking her questions about some journal."

"What kind of building are they keeping her in?"

"It looks like an old livery stable, but there ain't no horses there anymore, and the doors are barred."

"It's a wonder you didn't run holes in your shoes, my boy, all that chasing you did. I shall have to buy you new ones—and give you a nice reward for your bravery." It was best that Devere keep talking, or else he'd go mad with worry about Caroline.

With every clop of hooves, he prayed he wouldn't be too late, prayed the men wouldn't harm her. Time was their enemy. He had to get there before they did the unspeakable.

The darker it became, the fewer conveyances crowded the streets.

From the Strand, they wove through a nest of dark, narrow lanes of dilapidated houses. Babes cried. Elderly women cackled. Gin-soaked men sprawled on the pavement. He marveled that Billy had found his way back to Mayfair from here. And he hoped like hell the lad could find that old livery stable.

> ⤷⤺

THOSE VILE MEN who stank of onions had removed the gag from her mouth but not the rough ropes that cut into her wrists and ankles or the rope that tied her to a crude wooden chair. A single tallow lighted the dark, musty building.

"Where's the journal?" the older man barked.

"I don't know what you're talking about."

"Betsy Wyndham's journal."

"I don't know a Mrs. Wyndham."

The man drew his arm back, then slapped her face with such force, it knocked her backward.

Tears pricked. Her face stung. Her head began to throb.

"Violence cannot produce something that doesn't exist," she said. "I've never heard of a Mrs. Wyndham."

The younger of the vile men said, "She might be tellin' the truth. Considerable time has passed since the old lady died, and no one has made any demands."

Her captors had to be acting for someone else. Betsy Wyndham would have crossed the street to keep from breathing the same air as these two unsavory men.

Were it not for the fact the journal was in Lord Devere's library, she would have handed it over to them in the hopes of sparing her life—not that it would matter to these killers. They meant to kill her just as Betsy Wyndham had been killed. Even if she did give them the journal.

If she told them its hiding place, she'd be endangering Lord Devere. She'd lay down her life before she would do that.

"It's time to make her talk," the older man said with a sneer and a gleeful look in his eyes.

Torture. She prayed she would be strong enough to protect Lord Devere.

"It be in the next block, my lord." Billy pointed to a faded red brick building on the right side of the narrow street. It was unmistakably a livery stable. Or, it used to be one. There wasn't another horse around.

They dismounted, and Devere lowered his voice. "Stay with the horses," he instructed the lad. "And be especially quiet."

Devere moved like a cat toward the building. Obviously, he couldn't enter through the wide, barred front door. Then he spotted a slender door on the opposite side of it. He came to the door and tried to open it, but it was locked. He paused to listen.

"Gag her again," a man said. "We don't want no one to hear her screams."

It was all Devere could do not to rush into the building at that instant.

The next words he heard were enough to curdle his blood.

"We'll take the gag off as soon as you tell us to quit by raising your hand, but you cannot tell us to quit until you're ready to give up the damned book."

"I can't raise my hand. You tied it yourself!"

"Then nod your head, damn woman!"

Devere had to get in there. "Go try the back door," he ordered Frederick. He then unsheathed a knife from his boot and worked at the rusty lock until it crumbled. He tried the door, just an inch, to see if he'd succeeded. Relief rushed over him when it opened. Then he stooped down and prepped his pistol, got to his feet, and slammed the door open.

CHAPTER FOURTEEN

CAROLINE'S BACK WAS to the door, so she couldn't see who was busting into this old building, but an explosive sound shook her chair and hurt her ears. Before she could make out that it came from a firearm, the knife her captor was threatening her with fell to the floor. The foul man fell backward, clutching his chest. Crimson soaked his dingy shirt.

Her head swung around. Lord Devere. Pistol in one hand, his drawn sword in the other and his face twisted with rage, he rushed toward her second captor.

Lord Devere was the most magnificent sight she had ever beheld.

As the earl came closer to him, fear transformed the second man's face. Then he whirled around and ran toward the back door like a kitten chased by a big dog. Lord Devere went after him but returned a moment later with Frederick, locking the door behind him and shaking his head gravely.

"He was too quick for me," Frederick said. "The blighter disappeared into the darkness."

"We need to get you out of here at once," Devere said to Caroline. He knelt beside the man who'd been shot and felt for a pulse. "He's gone." He looked up at his footman. "You'll need to come back with help to properly dispatch this vile creature. Go have Billy bring up the horses now."

She was sure it was a sin to be pleased over someone's death, but she couldn't help but to feel freed from certain death at the dead man's hands. Her sense of relief was palpable. That horrid man couldn't hurt her again.

She understood why Lord Devere wanted to whisk her away immediately. Reinforcements could be coming—reinforcements which could outnumber him and be better armed. The very thought of Lord Devere being injured, or even killed, in her defense crushed her with guilt.

He extracted his knife and cut the ropes that tied her to the rickety chair. Then, as he slashed through the ropes that bound her hands and feet, he cursed. "What kind of savages would do this to a defenseless woman?" Her broken skin oozed blood. His voice gentled. "Have they hurt you in any other way?"

Like a kettle building steam, the fear and worry of the past two hours had risen to the point where she could no longer contain her exploding emotions. Tears began to gush as she shook her head. "I'm unhurt."

Still kneeling at her feet, he drew her into his firm embrace. "Thank God, Caroline. For that single moment I thought you were . . . dead, I could not bear it."

Everything she'd been through was worth this moment. She slipped from the chair to her knees and held him firmly, torso to torso. This most wondrous man cared for her! She gloried in the way she felt in his arms. Not only did he make her feel safe and protected, but she was also swamped by this closeness to this man she adored. They were so close his breath puffed on the sensitive skin of her neck. She could feel the heat of him, smell his musky scent.

She longed to tell him she loved him, but that would be too presumptuous. Also, expressing herself, especially her feelings, had never come easily to her.

He pressed light kisses into her hair and traced sultry circles on her back, then he pulled away ever so gently and peered at her, smoothing away the remnants of her tears with the pads of his thumbs. "We need to talk."

She nodded solemnly. "I'm so sorry."

He got to his feet and then helped her up.

Just outside the door, their horses awaited. "Billy's responsible for saving your life, Miss Rutherford."

Her gaze ran over the slender lad who was about twelve years of age. He dressed nattily in buckskin breeches that tucked into spotless top boots, narrow coat, and gold-corded cap. "What a brave lad you are! Words are inadequate to express how deeply indebted I am to you, Billy," she said.

"The master says as how he's gonna give me a reward, miss."

"I am very indebted to our master, too. He is also very brave."

To her great satisfaction, Lord Devere had her ride back to Mayfair on the same horse as he rode. Her back spooning into him, she took comfort in his arms at either side of her.

As happy as she was over her rescue and especially at having won Lord Devere's affection, she knew she was going to have to confess to him that she was living a lie, that she had lied to him since the first day.

She must prepare herself for being tossed out of his house.

HIS SISTER MUST have been hovering at the window because she flew into Caroline's arms as soon as they entered the house. "Did those awful men hurt you?"

"No. Thanks to your brother's bravery."

"I did what any man would do when his family is threatened."

"See, Miss Rutherford, I told you Devere would always treat you as if you were a member of our family."

He effected a stern look at his sister. "You may go to your chamber now, young lady. I must speak to Miss Rutherford."

Harriett gave him a contrite look and bowed her head. "I'm being scolded for my wickedness." She returned her attention to Miss Rutherford. "I am powerless to convey to you how truly sorry I am for being responsible for the horrible things that happened to you."

Miss Rutherford shook her head. "I beg you not to blame yourself. How were you to know evil men were watching us? I'm just happy you were spared."

"She's right, Harry. It's not your fault, but you're still to be punished for disobeying me."

Harriett hung her head and began to climb the stairs. On the third step, she turned back. "I'm so happy you're unhurt, Miss Rutherford."

In his candlelit library, he and Caroline sat on the sofa. There was no fire this night. It had been a warm day. "You owe me an explanation."

She nodded. A moment passed before she gathered her words. "My name is not Caroline Rutherford. It's Charlotte Robinson. My real father was the Honorable Matthew . . ."

"Robinson. I admired him very much. I was very sorry to learn of the fire. But, of course, it doesn't explain why you changed your identity." The intelligence she'd just conveyed explained so much and vindicated him for his suspicions, but it did not vindicate her.

"Did I not read in the newspapers that Matthew Robinson's daughter was culpable in the murder of Mrs. Betsy Wyndham?"

"I'll explain. After the fire, being without resources, I went into service as a companion for a wealthy woman in Devon. She was very kind to me. I didn't know until her murder that she had been a Cyprian."

"You speak of Betsy Wyndham?"

"Yes. Sometime before her death, she had given me a letter and a small book to keep. She asked me not to look at them unless she died."

"Did you really not look?"

"I still haven't read the book, which appears to be a journal. I read the letter the night I found her body."

"So you did not kill her?"

Her eyes watered. "I loved her. She was good to me."

"But she was murdered?"

"Yes."

"Do you know by whom?"

"No."

"What did her letter say?"

"It indicated I might be in danger. I fled Devon that very night."

"With the journal?"

"Yes."

"So when her body was discovered, and you were missing, others assumed you had done the deed?"

"Yes."

"How long ago was that?"

"Just before I came to London."

"This year?"

"Yes. I realized the murderer might think I could identify him—which I couldn't—so, to save my life, I decided to change my name."

"But what about Miss Fletcher? She's one of the most reputable people I've ever dealt with. How could you fool her?"

"Actually, she orchestrated my plan to change my name, supply me with bogus reference, and to come here—though I truly believe she's uncorruptible. She did this for me because of a family connection between us. Her sister was my beloved childhood nurse."

He was relieved that his faith in Miss Fletcher had not been misplaced. "The plan should have been as safe as the queen's jewels. How do you think you were discovered?"

"I have no idea. I will own, I was terrified of discovery that night at the Hollands' when Sir Andrew remembered having met me. I should never have gone to Holland House. My father was

too entrenched in government for me not to have met many
Members of Parliament. I should have known better than to
continue in those same circles, though that's where my interests
have always lain."

"Had you gone to Almack's when you were Charlotte Robinson?"

"Just a few times. Though my father was a gentleman, his
income was fairly modest, and we certainly were not members of
the *ton*."

"So going to Almack's probably did not unmask your real
identity."

"Probably not." She shook her head ruefully. "I refuse to
believe the murderer is a Whig."

He burst out laughing. "We Whigs, you know, are not infal-
lible. And just because the murderer may have learned your
identity from your appearance at Holland House doesn't mean
he's a Whig."

"I'm so sorry for endangering you and Lady Harriett. I had
planned to leave Devere House after my room was searched
because I knew that meant the murderer had found me, and I
didn't want to jeopardize you and your sister." She shut her eyes
tightly. "Especially after I caused Jonathan's death."

"It's not your fault he was killed. None of this has been your
fault. You were merely trying to stay alive." He lifted her hand
and kissed the back of it. "I, for one, am grateful you're still alive."

"You're not angry that I lied?"

"No. I applaud you for the courage you demonstrated. It has
to have been difficult to turn your back on everything and
everyone you've known and start a new identity."

"But think how I've endangered you and your sister."

"Not your fault. Now answer this: Why did those men not
find the journal in your chamber?"

"Because it's not there."

"Did you leave it in Miss Fletcher's care?"

"No. It's here in this chamber. That's another reason I've felt so beastly about endangering you. Those men were about to torture me to learn its location. Had I been too weak to withstand it, what would have happened to you if they came here for it?"

"But, thankfully, my arrival prevented the torture, and only the two of us know where it is."

"I've been thinking about Mrs. Wyndham's journal. Mrs. Wyndham is my former employer who was murdered."

"Just to confirm, you are speaking of Betsy Wyndham?"

"You knew her?"

"I never met her, but I knew of her. In addition to her inamoratas, she possessed a prominent box at Theatre Royal, and most of us used to gawk at the woman. I remember when I first came down from Oxford, I thought she was beautiful." His tone turned more serious. "Tell me everything you can remember about her death."

"Though she had obviously retired when she settled in Devon, on occasion she would entertain callers. I realize now they must have been men. She was always mysterious about it. She maintained another home on the other side of the village for her servants' use, and on these nights, she would always send away all the servants."

"You, too?"

"No. Like you, she never treated me like a servant. Since my chamber was in a wing on the opposite side of the house from Mrs. Wyndham's, she would merely request that I not leave my room on the nights the callers came."

"Did she say anything about who that last caller was?"

"Not at all."

"And you discovered her body the night she was killed, or was it later?"

"That night. I'd heard a noise and went to investigate."

"What kind of noise?"

"At the time, I wasn't sure. I realize now it was Mrs. Wyndham's . . . death cry."

His brows lowered. "And when you went to investigate, you

saw nothing of the killer?"

"I didn't know it at the time, but I saw a shadowy figure. He left the house by way of the main entrance."

"Think. What do you remember about him?"

"Nothing really. I had just reached the ground floor and was moving to the staircase that led to Mrs. Wyndham's wing. The ground floor lights had all been extinguished, so it was very dark. I wouldn't even have seen him had he not opened the entrance door and fled into the night. I could not say what his hair color was or anything about him, other than he dressed as a man. He was of average build and probably average height, but without standing near him, I couldn't even be certain of that."

"I expect at that time your concern was for Mrs. Wyndham."

"It was. I sped to her chambers and found her. Dead. She was dressed as would one going to bed, and she had obviously been strangled. Her bedchamber and its adjoining study had both been searched." Caroline's eyes shut tightly. Her recollections must be painful. "It was left in the same disarray as my chamber here was." She looked up at him. "They killed Jonathan."

She felt worse over his footman's death than he did. The fellow had not deserved to die, but he had brought it on himself.

"It's my belief the person who killed Mrs. Wyndham is likely prominent in some way in London. He must have hired those two men who abducted you. Here in the Capital, he wouldn't be able to risk discovery over his dirty deeds."

"Those men told me they were the ones who searched my chamber."

"And they also showed great interest in learning the location of the journal, did they not?"

"They did."

"That means something in her journal threatens Mrs. Wyndham's killer in some way."

"So, if we read the journal, we might discover his identity?"

"Correct."

"I feel foolish to admit it now, but it never occurred to me

Mrs. Wyndham's callers were men. Well, what I mean is, I thought the callers might be men, but it never occurred to me the visits might be . . . of a personal nature."

He tried to stifle a smile. "That's because you're an innocent."

She did not respond for a moment, and when she did, he was astonished at what she said. "I never feel innocent when . . . I'm with you." Her lashes lowered, and he could tell it embarrassed her to admit something so personal.

God, but he wanted to devour her. Right now. In this library. He throbbed with need for this woman. But he had to be strong. This was not the time to seek his own pleasure. Not when her life was in danger. She was too precious to him.

He took both her hands and kissed them, refusing to let go. "You must never feel ashamed of these feelings. I have them, too, toward you. But right now, we must direct our attentions to doing everything in our power to locate Betsy Wyndham's murderer. Until we do, you will never be safe."

He turned her hands palms up and pressed kisses into the more sensitive flesh there. "And nothing's more important to me than protecting those I . . . care about."

Her gaze lifted to him. Candlelight flickered in her honeyed brown hair. "Thank you for saving my life. I wish to spend the rest of my life in service to you."

He could groan with want. He was beginning to think he wanted her for the rest of his life, too, but such an important decision could not be taken lightly.

He cleared his throat. "Will you fetch the journal now?"

CHAPTER FIFTEEN

CAROLINE STOOD ON her toes to reach the shelf and remove several volumes in order to get the journal that had been dropped in back of them. She had to rely on her hands because she wasn't tall enough to see the shelf.

"Do you need help?" he asked, moving toward her.

"Perhaps I do."

He retrieved the slim volume and gave it to her.

She looked up at him. "We'll read it together." It felt so liberating to be able to share the heavy burden that had crushed her these past weeks.

When they returned to the sofa, he scooted next to her, his gaze falling to the book in her lap. "You really had no curiosity to know its contents?"

"I cannot say I had no curiosity. I did not pry because I respect other's privacy."

"That's remarkable, considering you're a female."

"How dare you malign my gender," she said flippantly.

"I do beg your forgiveness. My perceptions of your gender are colored by knowledge of my sisters, who may not be reflective of all females."

"I believe your sisters are far more representative of other females than I."

He chuckled. "I must agree. You, Miss Rutherford, are singular."

Her lashes lowered as she began to flip the pages. The first page with Mrs. Wyndham's scratchy handwriting was dated some sixteen years previously. "Should I read aloud, or do we each read silently?"

"Let's just silently scan."

"Good."

Once she had learned of Mrs. Wyndham's sullied past, Caroline assumed the journal would be an enumeration of the woman's amorous conquests. She still felt guilty prying into such personal details.

On the first page Mrs. Wyndham wrote that she had received a settlement of two hundred a year from Lord Chaney upon his marriage to his youthful bride. The baron's marriage was an apparent love match, and his betrothed had demanded that he sever ties with his mistress.

Caroline remembered watching Lord and Lady Chaney dance at Lady Jersey's ball and thinking how in love they appeared.

She flipped on to the next entry, less than a month later. Mrs. Wyndham's new protector was Sir Arthur Hawes. According to what the woman had written, Sir Arthur was some twenty years her senior and not attractive, but he was kindly and generous. The next several pages discussed her activities ranging from new dresses to plays she attended but made for dull reading.

While still being under Sir Arthur's protection, Mrs. Wyndham had a brief but torrid affair with the youngest son of the Duke of Tatum. Caroline's cheeks stung as she began to read about a particularly lusty encounter. She quickly turned the page, but she was unable to purge from her thoughts the words *I could have lain with my sweet Johnny all night and all of the next day for nothing has ever felt better than feeling him inside of me.*

Mrs. Wyndham was saddened when her sweet Johnny returned to the North Country.

She wrote of tiring of Sir Arthur and of looking for a replacement.

Then, about a fourth of the way into the journal, an astonishing passage jolted Caroline.

Though I've long gone by the name of Mrs. Wyndham, I never married any Mr. Wyndham. I am still legally the wife of a man I've come to loathe. At the age of sixteen, I secretly married a younger son of Lord Atwell. He soon tired of me, and paid for my silence about our marriage. At the time, it was more money than I'd ever seen, but I realize now if I'd insisted on recognition of our marriage, I would have fared much better. He eventually wed an heiress. So now I am the only person who knows he is not legally married to his heiress. And since then, I've made him pay for my silence. I aim to be one of the richest women in the kingdom. And from now on, only men of my choosing will be permitted into my bed.

After reading the passage, Caroline's astonished gaze met Lord Devere's.

"That's our murderer," he said.

"He certainly had powerful motivation. That secret marriage could nullify his marriage to the heiress."

"And make any children born of that union illegitimate. It's a solid motive for killing Betsy Wyndham—or whatever her real name was."

Caroline read over the passage once more. "She doesn't name him, other than to say he's a younger son of Lord Atwell. Do you know Lord Atwell?"

"There are ten thousand aristocrats in Britain. I can't possibly know them all, but it so happens one Lord Atwell does, on the rare occasion, sit in the House of Lords, though I've never spoken to him. He's quite elderly."

"Do you have any knowledge of how many sons he has?"

He stood. "I may not, but the information ought to be in my *Burke's*." He went to his bookshelves, located the fat peerage volume, and returned to sit beside her. This time, the book was on his lap, and he turned to the page where Atwells were listed.

"Here it is." His index finger stayed on the listing for the Earl of Atwell, whose family seat was Dannerly in Hertfordshire. Their family name was Wilson.

The print was too small for her to easily read from this distance, especially by dim candlelight.

"The current earl, who inherited in1790, has four sons and six daughters," he said. "The eldest son is named John; next, Robert; the third goes by Sinclair; and the youngest was given the name Samuel. According to the dates of their births, the youngest is five years older than me."

"Then I don't suppose you know any of the Wilson brothers?"

"You will be happy to learn I don't think they're Whigs."

She grinned. "How can you possibly speculate that?"

"I've never seen them at Brooks'."

The club frequented by Whigs. "How can we find out which son married an heiress?"

"First, we have to consider what constitutes an heiress. It's possible that a youthful Betsy Wyndham would have considered any woman with a large dowry to be an heiress, and I dare say no son of the Earl of Atwell would be permitted to marry a woman who did not bring a generous dowry to the marriage."

"As disheartening as it is, I do suppose you're right." She sighed. "Each of the Wilson brothers likely wed well-dowered women."

"Our first step is to find the brothers."

"How do you propose to do that?" she asked.

"I'm not sure. I'll start by asking Alex if there are any Wilsons serving in the House of Commons."

That made her recall that her father was a bit of a rarity in the House of Commons, which was populated by sons of peers. "And even if only one of the brothers is, that could lead to the other three, would it not?"

"How clever you are, Miss Rutherford."

Flattery from the queen herself could not have met with

more glee than the slightest morsel of praise from the Earl of Devere. She did prefer it when his lordship called her *Caroline*—even if it wasn't her real name—but knew he only used that as an endearment during intimate moments. She respected that his determination to stop the murderer took precedence over furthering his own romantics interests. If they were romantic.

"Is it too late tonight to contact Mr. Muir?" she asked.

"I'll go see him now."

ALEX WAS NOT at his home on Half Moon Street, which meant there was a good likelihood the session at the House of Commons had gone well into the night, a not uncommon occurrence.

Devere went directly to the Palace of Westminster's St. Stephen's Chapel. He'd not been to the House of Commons since he'd briefly served there upon reaching the requisite age of one-and-twenty. His father's death the following year had sent him to the House of Lords.

He easily spotted Alex on one of the front benches and went to him. A young man Devere did not know was in the process of delivering an impassioned address, but no one seemed to be paying the slightest attention to him, and Devere could not for the life of him determine what the topic of his speech was.

"What the devil are you doing here, old boy?" Alex asked.

"If it's not too much of an imposition, I'd like to speak to you on a matter of a private nature."

Alex stood. "Let's go into the corridor."

Once away from the noisy chamber, Devere weighed how much he was willing to tell his closest friend. They had never kept secrets from one another and, frankly, Devere could use all the help he could get to prevent a potential murder.

"Why is it I fear you're going to tell me you've become smitten with Miss Rutherford and plan to marry her?" Alex said.

The comment shocked Devere. Marry Caroline? It wasn't done. Men from his class plucked brides from among their own. Yet . . . contemplating possessing Caroline was as pleasant to his two-and-thirty-year-old self as stuffing his ten-year-old self with plum pudding had been. Even more so. "Why would you say that?"

"It's obvious I'm smitten with her—just as obvious as it is that you, too, have been snared by Cupid's arrow. I thought you might feel the need to announce I was no longer in the running for her hand. Being my oldest friend, and all that."

His best friend knew him better than he knew himself. "I have not come to tell you I'm going to marry Miss Rutherford."

Muir eyed Devere suspiciously. "I fear, old boy, you have fallen under the lady's spell, and I certainly understand the attraction. She's most singular, to be sure. Not at all like the others one meets." He sighed. "I have come to realize I cannot consider marrying her. Unlike you, I have not the luxury of marrying a woman without a dowry."

"I've come to you because her life is in danger, and . . ."

Fury blazed across Alex's face. "Danger? What's happened?"

"Permit me to explain." Devere threw an arm around his friend as they strode the length of the corridor. "Miss Rutherford, I've just learned, is not Miss Rutherford."

"Who is she?"

"Do you remember Matthew Robinson?"

"Of course. Such a tragedy. And his son perished with him. Very sad. And such a loss to the Whigs. But what does this have to do with Miss Rutherford?"

"Her real name is Charlotte Robinson, the daughter of Matthew Robinson. She was forced to change her name to protect herself. She's in possession of information which poses a great threat to a man who wishes to permanently silence her." Devere drew a long breath. "I managed to save her from cutthroats tonight, but her life is by no means out of danger."

"Good lord! Who's the man?"

"We're not certain, but we believe it to be one of the four sons of the Earl of Atwell. The family name is Wilson. Do you know them?"

"I don't know the earl, but there's a Wilson serving in the House of Commons."

"That's why I'm here. What's his first name?"

"John."

"A Tory?"

"Yes."

"Good."

"Why is that good?"

"Neither Miss Rutherford—or Robinson—nor I would wish for the murderer to be a Whig."

A deep chuckle rose in Alex's chest. "Now I understand why the lady's so passionate toward our cause. Her father's contributions can never be forgotten." He shook his head. "I need to know more about this. Murderer, as in one who kills?"

"Yes. He's already killed twice, and Miss Rutherford will be next if we don't stop him."

"We certainly must stop him. Who, pray tell, did he murder?"

During the next ten minutes, as they paced the corridor, Devere filled him in on all things to do with Betsy Wyndham and Caroline's trail to London, including the murder of his own footman.

"Good God, man! What can I do to help?"

Devere moved to return to the chapel where the House of Commons was meeting. "You can point out John Wilson. That will be a start."

"He's a back bencher. About five-and-forty years of age."

Inside the chamber, Alex pointed out the eldest son of Lord Atwell. The man was slightly portly with a balding head fringed with gray tufts. Caroline's glimpse of the murderer that night in Devon revealed that he was of average build, not portly. But, of course, this was the eldest son. The heir. The murderer, the man Betsy Wyndham married, was a younger son. Devere nodded and lowered his voice. "You must befriend him. And quickly."

"Then what?"

"We've got to know where each of his brothers are and if any of the Wilsons have married an heiress."

"A tall order, to be sure."

"If possible, tonight."

"I was thinking of inviting him to my club to discuss the bill on penal reform or the Civil List or something we members are weighing in on, but I'm sure he's not a member of Brooks', and I no longer belong to White's."

"Beg the fellow to accompany you to Brooks'."

"Devere, you must come with us. You're much better at impressing people than I. I dare say you could have the fellow eating from your hand."

"Very well."

CHAPTER SIXTEEN

"I THINK YOU need a plan," Devere said to Alex. "You're well respected in this chamber. Honor him. Say you've been watching him for some time, and he's just the man for . . . whatever legislation is important right now, but don't have it be anything too radical or progressive, in case he's not bent in that direction."

"Right-o! What about tightening the reins on the regent's spending? Everyone agrees with that."

"That should work."

The two men made their way to the second-to-last bench where John Wilson appeared to be the only person in the room listening enthusiastically to the speaker. The man was impeccably dressed in a freshly starched shirt and cravat of snow white, finely tailored coat of high-quality black wool, and gray pantaloons that were becoming the latest rage among men of fashion. What little hair he possessed had been styled in the most flattering way possible, and each of his slightly pudgy hands sported manly rings with sizable diamonds. While he could not control nature's shortcomings, Mr. John Wilson slaved to control everything else about his appearance.

Devere stood just behind Alex as he initiated conversation with Wilson. "Forgive me, sir, for interrupting. It appears you're interested in Barton's talk. Do you know the young man?"

Only previous acquaintance could account for such an interest, Devere thought.

"No, Mr. Muir, but I have a great interest in cultivating young men who are only beginning to make their way in the world. I often take them under my wing, so to speak."

Wilson's statement was all the more remarkable, thought Devere, because of the effete manner in which he spoke. A *girly man*, to be sure. Of course Alex, who never thought ill of anyone, would be oblivious to such signs.

"How commendable," Alex said. "You're just the sort of man I've been seeking. Pray, sir, could I persuade you to come to Brooks' now with me and my friend, Lord Devere?"

Wilson shot an inscrutable look at Devere, then answered. "I should be honored."

"We can all go in Devere's coach." Alex turned to Devere. "It is standing at the ready outside, is it not?"

"It is."

In the coach, Alex sat next to Wilson for the short drive to St. James' Street. Devere lamented that Wilson's company on the ride would prevent him and Alex the opportunity to devise a solid plan.

On St. James' Street, the coach pulled up in front of the club to which the last three generations of Deveres—and all the Whig grandees—had belonged for three-quarters of a century. Inside, they found a quiet corner, and the waiter soon brought them brandy.

"I'd like to propose a toast," Alex said, looking at John Wilson. "To forging a new relationship."

Wilson's twinkling pale blue eyes never left Alex's as their glasses touched. Devere's glass was later tapped as an afterthought.

"Bringing you here to Brooks' in no way means I'm trying to foist my beliefs upon my new friend," Alex said to that new friend, "but it's the only club to which I hold membership. Now, I'd like to know a bit more about you. Tell me, is there a Mrs. Wilson?"

The corners of Wilson's mouth lifted to a smile. "No. I've never married. Got three brothers, so I believe the succession of the Atwell title is secure without my contribution."

"Oh," Devere interrupted, "your brothers have started their families, then?"

"Yes. Each has at least one son."

And one of those brothers had an illegitimate son or sons.

Wilson redirected his attentions to Alex. Devere was quite certain the man moved his chair closer to Alex, too. "I dare say you've not married, either, Mr. Muir. I could see we have much in common."

"Yes, it's true. I'm a bachelor, free to follow my heart whichever direction it takes me."

Good lord, did Alex not see he was inadvertently giving amorous encouragement to this man?

"I have a confession," Wilson said, eyeing Alex.

"Do you now?"

"Indeed. I have long admired you."

Devere felt compelled to intervene. "You are not alone, Mr. Wilson. My friend is widely admired for his many contributions to our government. Indeed, even my sister and her companion are enthusiastic admirers of him."

"You both are too kind," Alex said.

Devere once again addressed Wilson. "So, Wilson, you are an uncle?"

"I am."

"I am, too," Alex said. "Just one more thing you and I have in common."

Devere wished there was some way he could have communicated with his unsuspecting friend who was playing into this man's flirtation. He eyed Wilson. "Isn't it remarkable that three brothers can so rapidly expand one's family? You've now got nieces and nephews and sisters-in-law. By the way, do you get along with your brothers' wives?"

"As well as can be expected. I doubt if anyone gets along with

Robert's wife. She was raised to vast expectations, and I dare say she thinks anything less than a duke unworthy of her. Makes his life difficult."

"Vast expectations because of her own wealth?" Alex questioned.

"Yes. She was the only child and sole heir of a disgustingly wealthy beer merchant."

Ah, they had their man! "I suppose, unless they have a house in London, you don't have to see her much," Devere said.

"Oh, they do live in London, but I don't see them often. At least, not as much I see Samuel and his wife. Now, Sam's wife's an heiress, too, but you'd never know it. A sweeter lady you'd never find."

Two heiresses? That certainly complicated matters. Devere and Alex exchanged somber glances.

"Then Samuel's here in London, too?" Devere asked.

"Yes." Wilson's gaze went to Alex. "Permit me to pour you more brandy, my dear fellow."

"Don't tell me all three of your brothers have wed heiresses," Devere said playfully.

Wilson shook his head. "No, poor Sinclair has to manage on the same income as I do, but our father is as generous as he's able to be. He's on in years now, and it's only a matter of time before I'll be the new Earl of Atwell—not that I wish to hasten that day. My father's an excellent parent."

"Another thing we have in common." Alex was feeding into this man's misconceptions. "My parent is also along in years, and I don't think it will be long before I inherit his title. Of course, a mere baron is not as lofty as an earl, like Lord Devere."

Wilson's chair moved closer to Alex. "What a fateful night this is for us."

Alex seemed perplexed over this last comment but soon responded. "It's quite remarkable that we've served in the House of Commons together all these years and not come to know one another as we are tonight."

Devere meant to get back to his vital line of inquiry. "And where do you reside, Mr. Wilson?"

Wilson stared admiringly at Alex as he answered in a low, seductive voice. "I have lodgings at Albany."

"And your brothers," Devere continued, "they live close to you?"

"They do. Sinclair is at our country seat, but Samuel and Robert are both right in Mayfair. I can walk to each of their houses." Wilson's gaze shifted from Devere to Alex. "And where is your home?"

"As it happens, I could easily walk to your house. I'm on Half Moon Street."

Though Wilson had no interest in him, Devere interjected his comment once more. "And I'm on Curzon Street. So we're all rather close. Are there any Wilsons on my street—or perhaps on Alex's?"

"Not to my knowledge," Wilson answered. "I say, Devere, that's a fine coat you're wearing. Can spot a Weston anywhere."

"Thank you." Devere decided to abandon his efforts to find out where Wilson's brothers lived. There were other ways of locating them. Now he needed to determine which of them had secretly married Betsy Wyndham. Since she'd written that she's been just sixteen, there was a good likelihood that her husband wasn't a great deal older. If only she would have said where the marriage occurred or where she'd met her husband, he would have had more clues to trace the man's identity.

"I know my clothing is not as fashionable as yours or Lord Devere's," Alex said.

Wilson directed his comments to Alex once more. "One who's as brilliant a parliamentarian as you, my dear fellow, has many other more important attributes than an eye for fashion. Look how often you're mentioned in the newspapers. Why, I feel positively honored to be sitting here with you tonight."

"I perceive," Devere said to the man, "you were far too serious minded to engage in flirtations while at university, but what of your brothers? I expect they were quite the skirt chasers."

"How perceptive you are, my lord. I most certainly did not mingle with light skirts when I was at Cambridge."

"It was the same with me," Alex said. "I took my studies most seriously."

Why in the devil was Alex being so blasted dense? Had he forgotten the purpose of their mission?

"And you still do, only the nature of what you now study has changed," Wilson complimented.

Devere needed to get Wilson talking about his brothers. "I would wager your brothers weren't as interested in their studies as you, Wilson."

"You would win your wager. Yes, they were quite the skirt chasers. Especially Robert. He actually lived for a time with a pretty little thing. Not of our class, of course."

This was promising. Devere tried to recall what Betsy Wyndham looked like. She was very fair, with pale blonde hair, and her figure—even as she aged—was perfection. "I suppose she was a dark-haired siren?"

Wilson shook his head. "Not at all. She was possessed of blonde hair. Met her once. I managed to persuade Robert to give her a small settlement and be done with her. And I proved to be right about the tart. She later made rather a name for herself as a courtesan here in London."

"Rather reminds me of Betsy Wyndham," Devere said.

"That's the very one!"

Devere stood. "As pleasant as this has been, I've just remembered Muir and I have a previous commitment."

Alex stood. "Oh, yes, I quite forgot."

"We must meet again," Wilson said to Alex. "May I call on you at Half Moon Street?"

"Certainly."

Wilson stood. "I shall need a lift back to the Palace of Westminster where my gig is."

"Oh, yes, of course."

After Wilson had been dropped off, Alex said, "Jolly nice fellow. So glad he's not the murderer."

"Of course he was being nice to you! The fellow thinks you've selected him to be your special friend."

"Isn't that what we decided when inviting him to Brooks'?"

"When I say *special*, I refer to a certain proclivity . . . you remember old Yarwood from Oxford?"

The coach went dead silent. "You don't mean . . ."

"Yes. Did you not notice his chair kept scooting closer to you, and that he only had eyes for you?"

"Dear lord! And I kept saying as how we had so much in common! The man's bound to think I'm . . . well, like him!"

"That's exactly what he thinks, my friend. You kept telling him how very much alike you two were."

Alex tightly shut his eyes. "And he's to call on me at Half Moon Street. What am I to do?"

"Tell him you're in love and contemplating marriage. Don't worry about John Wilson now. It's his murdering brother who is our concern."

"You know you can't just go about accusing the brother without some kind of proof."

"Yes, I know. But how in the devil can I get my hands on proof?"

"There is the woman's journal."

"But he's not named in it."

"That is a bit of a problem. Perhaps you could find the surviving cutthroat from Miss Rutherford's abduction."

"A tall order, given that London's the largest city in the world. It's not likely such a man is in my social sphere."

"True."

Devere perked up. "I know!"

"What?"

"The registry at the church!"

"Of course. The marriage had to have been recorded there. But where, precisely, is it?"

"I don't actually know. Perhaps Miss Rutherford will."

"If the lady has heard it, she will remember. Uncommon memory. Intelligent, too. By the way, drop me off at Half Moon Street. I need a good night's sleep. I'm to meet with the Chancellor of the Exchequer tomorrow morning."

"I am honored to have a man as important as you as my friend."

After Alex left the coach, he turned back. "I stand ready to help you and Miss Rutherford."

"I know."

When Devere arrived home, Miss Rutherford rushed to him.

He quickly glanced around. No one else was there. "Come, let's go to the library."

In the library, they went to the sofa. "What is my sister doing this evening?"

"She's beside herself with glee. The female dove laid two eggs, and Lady Harriett's fascinated to watch the male and female taking turns sitting upon the crudest nest you ever saw. She's quite in heaven. It was the best gift you could have given her. But now you must tell me if you learned anything about the Wilsons."

"Indeed I did."

"The identity of Mrs. Wyndham's killer?"

He nodded.

"Who, pray tell, is it?"

"The second son of Lord Atwell. One Robert Wilson." He went on to explain how he'd been able to determine the killer's identity but omitted the now-comical flirtation on the part of John Wilson. One did not discuss such a thing in front of a lady. It wouldn't surprise him if neither his sister nor Miss Rutherford had ever heard of that particular preference.

"Can we send the magistrates after him?"

"He's terribly wealthy. His wife was the sole heiress of her father's fortune made in brewing, and that kind of wealth can buy a lot. There's also the matter of proof. I doubt anyone would arrest him without a shred of proof."

"But we know he did it! He might even believe I saw him that night in Devon, the night he killed Mrs. Wyndham." She paused a moment, then added. "I know! Use me to set a trap."

"I would never permit that! Besides, I believe the incriminating evidence may lay in the registry at the church where he married Betsy Wyndham."

"Do you know where they married?"

"No, but since it was a secret wedding, my guess is that instead of being at his home parish, it would have been at hers. Surely, having been friend to the lady for a year, you know where she grew up."

"Actually, I do. She said she was from a little village in Middlesex." Miss Rutherford bit at her lip. "I'm trying to remember its name. Birkenfield! That's it."

Were Eardley not off in Shropshire investigating Miss Rutherford/Robinson, Devere would have sent him to investigate. "I will go there tomorrow."

"Please, may I come with you?"

He thought about it for a moment before answering. "Yes. I don't like leaving you, not when that man's bent on silencing you. We'll leave in the morning." He wished Alex was coming with them, but one did not turn down a meeting with the Chancellor of the Exchequer—especially one possessed of political ambition.

CHAPTER SEVENTEEN

EVEN BEFORE DEVERE had the opportunity to apprise his sister of their journey to Middlesex, she was prevented from accompanying them by an unfortunate occurrence to their Great-aunt Margaret. The septuagenarian sent around a note to Harriett that morning, begging her to come assist the elderly lady, who had twisted her ankle the previous night. Of course, his tenderhearted sister had her bag packed immediately and hastened to Cavendish Square to help her infirm relation.

The intelligence that his sister would not accompany him awakened in him an eagerness to travel alone with the alluring Miss Rutherford. He was ashamed of his reaction, especially knowing the journey would require them to spend one night at an inn.

For propriety's sake, he knew he should not go off with Miss Rutherford without a chaperon, but it would be impossible to hire a chaperon at this late date. And hiring a chaperon for a chaperon was a most peculiar thing.

His greater concern was for Miss Rutherford's safety. He trusted no one else to look after her as well as he could. He would never forget the paralyzing fear that had seized him when he saw Harry sobbing and thought Caroline had been killed.

It had now been an hour and a half since he and Miss Rutherford had departed from Curzon Street in his traveling coach, and much of the noise of the metropolis had faded to only the passing saddle horse and the ringing of church bells in rural communities. Cognizant that they could be in danger, he had demanded that an armed groom sit on the box with the coachman for the duration of their journey.

Caroline sat opposite Devere, peering from the window on this sunny day.

"We are fortunate that Mrs. Wyndham did not grow up in Yorkshire," he said playfully.

Her soft green eyes twinkled as she regarded him. "Or Shropshire."

"Speaking of Shropshire, have you ever even been there?"

She shamefully shook her head. "Close. I'm from Cheshire. I cannot convey to you how dreadful the deception made me feel."

"Don't apologize. You did what anyone would have done to preserve her life against a murderer." He continued to regard her. "Now, I have a confession."

"I cannot believe that you, my lord, could possibly have done anything for which you would feel a compulsion to confess."

"Oh, but I did."

She sent him a quizzing gaze.

"I've sent my solicitor off to Shropshire."

"Whatever for?" As soon as she spoke, recognition lighted her face. "Oh, I see. You suspected all was not right about my falsified references. You must be very clever."

"I feel wretched admitting it. My suspicions had nothing to do with the most satisfactory performance of your duties."

"Was it Sir Andrew who gave me away?"

"I had my suspicions even before we went to Holland House that night."

"I do make a most inferior liar."

"Now that I've learned the facts, I've reflected back and realize you did your best to avoid telling lies. Is that why you've always been so quiet?"

"I suppose so. I was afraid if I talked, I would forget and incriminate myself. But you must tell me why you suspected my deception."

"Little things, like the failure to mention a single sibling when you professed to have so many." His voice gentled. "I am sincerely sorry for the loss of your real father and brother."

Her lashes lowered. "I miss them every day."

"And you couldn't even speak of them."

"Did something else alert you to my lies?"

"There was the fact your last employer was dead. Your father never stayed in one parish. And then there was the time you almost called yourself Charlotte."

"Then it's a very good thing I never met Mr. Robert Wilson."

"Indeed. I've been trying to think how he could have come to know you were living at my house under a false name. Do you have any ideas?"

"I did gather from those wretched men who would have killed me—had you not shown up—that their employer had sent them to Devon to learn all they could about me." She shrugged. "I never hid from those in Devon that I'd recently lost my entire family or that we'd lived in Romford-on-Mersey."

"Your father's home was in Romford-on-Mersey?"

"Yes, it's the village where I had lived for my whole life— except for the time we spent in London. Those vile men who abducted me said they'd been to my village, also."

"So they would have learned your father was an important Member of Parliament and that you'd spent much time in London. I expect that upon learning of your father's connection to Parliament, Wilson knew to look for you in London."

"But I still don't know how he could have traced me to your house. The only person—other than the unimpeachable Miss Fletcher—I ever saw in London who knew me from my old life was Sir Andrew, but Robert Wilson wouldn't have known to even question the man. And I would like to think that my denial to Sir Andrew was accepted. He is getting along in years, and I doubt his vision is all that good. It wasn't that brightly lit around the Hollands' table."

"I will own, I am stumped."

"The name of Caroline Rutherford did appear in the newspaper following that evening at Holland House."

"Knowing your father was a prominent Whig, Wilson could have suspected you'd naturally wish to resume the same activities that had absorbed you when your father was alive. There's a strong likelihood he'd have been reading accounts of anything that occurred at Holland House."

"You don't suppose he noticed that my initials were the same as Caroline Rutherford's?"

"That could be it."

They rode on in silence for a while before he said, "I'm going to have the devil of a time calling you Charlotte. You'll always be Caroline to me."

Her voice was barely above a whisper when she answered. "I blush to admit I have always fancied it when you called me Caroline."

"Then I won't change."

"It's not as if anyone else will hear."

As the sun rose directly above them, they stopped for a picnic in a meadow. On such a beautiful day, threats to this innocent woman and the murders of the Wyndham woman and his footman seemed to belong to another lifetime. Right now, with Caroline beside him, he could forget all the unpleasantness.

In one hand, he carried the basket his cook had packed with hard-cooked eggs, freshly baked bread, and cheeses from his home county. He had tucked in a bottle of wine, along with two glasses. In his other hand, he held hers.

How could such a simple act affect him mentally and physically so profoundly? For in spite of the gravity of today's mission and the peril which surrounded this young woman, he felt ten years younger. His step was light, his heart was gay, and he could not think of another place he would rather be than here at this moment with this special woman.

Then he realized this wasn't the first time he'd experienced such fulfilling happiness. The other time was also with Caroline.

She spread out the rug on the wild grass, and they sat next to each other, sloping, green hills and laconic sheep spread out before them for as far as the eye could behold. He began to empty the contents of the basket and poured wine for each of them.

"It's such a beautiful day," she said, taking the glass. "Thank you for allowing me to come."

He cupped her face. "You know I couldn't leave you. I protect what I care about."

Her misty gaze never leaving his, she set her hand atop his. "You're my rainbow after incredible bleakness."

He took her hand and tenderly kissed it. "I hope to always be there for you." He was getting far too intimate. "Now, for a toast." He lifted his glass. "May Robert Wilson be apprehended and pay for the crimes he's committed, and may Caroline be free to be herself, whether it be as Charlotte or Caroline."

She smiled and tapped his glass with her own.

They began to eat. It was simple fare, but it was a meal he would never forget. Because of her.

Nor could he remember when he'd ever desired any woman the way he desired Caroline. He would wager she had no notion of how her presence affected him.

After they ate, they strolled hand in hand while the youthful groom gathered the remnants of their meal and stashed the basket back in the coach. Neither Devere nor Caroline spoke. Their silence was a shared bond. Words weren't necessary on this most perfect of days.

Once they were back in the coach, he asked, "How much should we tell Harriett about you?"

"You will have to make that decision. I will say I'm beastly tired of living a lie."

"Then we'll tell her the truth. The entire truth. After Wilson's slated for the gallows."

"I pray she'll be safe today. I hated leaving her."

"Our great-aunt is a recluse. Harriett won't be leaving Cavendish Square, and we'll be back late tomorrow afternoon."

"She'll miss her creatures."

He smiled. "She'll miss you, too. It's remarkable how well the two of you get along." He could have looked far and wide across England and never found anyone more suited to handle his youngest sister than Caroline. He knew as certainly as he knew his sister that Caroline's fondness for Harry was genuine.

"I already miss her. I know I'm quite a bit older than Lady Harriett, but I feel almost as if I've gained a sister. It's helped me not miss my brother so horribly."

It took every ounce of strength he possessed not to pounce across that carriage, draw her into his loving embrace, and swear to do everything in his power to love her as she had once been loved by her family.

But he didn't love this woman as a brother loved his sister. He loved her as a man loves a woman.

Love? In his two-and-thirty years Devere had never been in love. Until Caroline came into his life. How could it be that he'd not actually realized he loved her until this moment? It was rather like the day he realized his father's hair had gone completely gray. It had come about so gradually, he'd not been aware of it until the transformation was total. Like this newly discovered love for Caroline.

His love had most certainly been building for several weeks, yet now the magnitude of his affection slammed into him with the force of a tidal wave. Now, he could no more deny that he loved her than he could turn his back on any of his sisters.

But what was he going to do about it?

She peered from the coach window. "We've come to a village that just might be Birkenfield."

He lifted the curtain to reveal a row of houses with low thatched roofs and doors so small he doubted he could pass through them without stooping. A short distance further along the high street, a sign for the King Charles Tavern and Inn swung in the gentle breeze.

He tapped the roof of the carriage for the coachman to stop. After the driver brought the vehicle to a stop and came around to open the coach door, Devere said, "Please inquire as to the name of this village."

A moment later, the coachman returned. "We be at Birkenfield. That was yer destination, was it not, my lord?"

Devere nodded as he eyed the wide, square steeple of the village's small church off in the distance. "Indeed it is." He stepped from the carriage, and then assisted Caroline in disembarking. "We'll start at the church, and you two men are free to go to the tavern while Miss Rutherford and I conduct our business here." He tossed a crown to the coachman.

Hand in hand once more, he and Caroline strolled to the village church and entered through its weathered door. On either side of the nave, a dozen rows of pews could accommodate no more than six or seven people each. The church was no larger than his family's Elizabethan chapel at Hamberly.

Even though it was an unusually sunny day, the interior of the church was dark. They went toward the altar. "No one's here. Perhaps we should try the rectory," he said. He had no intentions of poking about for the old registry without permission.

Upon leaving the tiny church, they passed a cemetery where it was almost impossible to read many of the inscriptions on leaning tombstones that had stood for centuries. Beyond that stood a modest red brick, four square house. "That has to be the rectory," he said.

He knocked on the door, which was soon answered by a young servant in a white mobcap. Devere handed her his card. "If this is the rectory, I should like to speak to the priest." He didn't know if the little church was served by a vicar, a rector, or even a curate. He was safer referencing him by the more generic *priest*.

"It is, my lord." She dipped into a curtsey. "Please do come in, my lord. I'll just go fetch Mr. Portman." She indicated for them to sit on side chairs set against the morning room wall.

A moment later, a bespectacled man who was roughly the same age as Devere entered the chamber, greeting them in a friendly manner. Devere had to hide his disappointment over the man's relative youth. It was unlikely he could have been the clergyman who performed the long-ago wedding ceremony between Betsy Wyndham and Robert Wilson.

"How can I serve you, my lord?" Mr. Portman asked.

Still standing after shaking the man's hand, Devere said, "We've come on a matter of grave importance. You might even say it's a matter of life or death. I can't go into details now, but—with your assistance—I should like to search through the parish registry for the record of a marriage that occurred about twenty years ago."

"Do you know the exact year?"

Devere shook his head. "I'm not even certain the marriage took place here, but we believe the bride was a member of your church, so we feel it likely they married here."

"Allow me to go get the keys, and we'll walk over to the church and search for the information you need."

When they reached the church, the clergyman led them to a small room off the sacristy. There, in a locked cabinet, he retrieved the aged book and set it upon a table. "Now what is the bride's name?"

Caroline answered. "I am not sure of her maiden name. She always went by the name Betsy, and she married a man named Robert Wilson."

Mr. Portman nodded as he flipped backward from the present day at least twenty pages. Using his index finger to mark the names, he eyed each entry. "This is for twenty years ago, but I see no Robert Wilson."

"Try the year before," Devere said.

He tried that. It took but a few seconds as only two couples wed that year, but neither was the pair they sought.

Devere moved closer so he, too, could see. "Go back another

year, if you please."

And there on the previous page in faded ink he clearly saw the names of Robert Wilson and Betsy Blunt.

"Ah, the Blunts! The last of them died this spring," the priest said.

"Mr. Portman, I would beg that you write a letter attesting to this marriage. This marriage may need to bear legal scrutiny."

"Certainly, my lord. Won't you come back to the rectory with me?" He returned the register to its cabinet and locked it.

As they strolled down the nave, the church's timbered door burst open, and there stood Caroline's surviving captor with a well-dressed gentleman Devere assumed to be Robert Wilson.

CHAPTER EIGHTEEN

CAROLINE HAD HOPED her path would never again cross with that of the filthy man who'd abducted her on Piccadilly. Now, here he stood, pointing a musket at her heart.

She lamented that the armed groom and coachmen were in the tavern and would never hear them if they were to call out for help.

Most of all, she lamented that she had endangered Lord Devere.

Her gaze flipped to the man beside the gunman. Dressed immaculately, the balding man in his mid-forties did not look like a murderer, but she had little doubt that he was the one who'd strangled the life from a woman he'd once loved.

Emboldened, Caroline moved closer, eyeing Robert Wilson with contempt. "So you're the fiend who killed Mrs. Wyndham." She made a snap decision not to admit that she would never have been able to identify him.

"And you, Miss Robinson, are the witness to my deed. You won't be permitted to live."

Now, Lord Devere stepped forward. "See here, Wilson, you can't kill all three of us with a single musket ball, and I vow to see that you pay for the Wyndham woman's death as well as the death of my faithful servant."

The unkempt man chortled. "Yer servant weren't so faithful.

For fifty quid, he allowed us into yer house that day, and he even stood watch."

Caroline did not condone what the footman had done, but she loathed what had been done to him. Evil men.

"He didn't deserve to die," Lord Devere snapped.

A smirk on his face, Wilson shrugged.

She addressed him. "What I've not been able to understand is how you persuaded Mrs. Wyndham to allow you into her house that night. She had to have known you wished her dead."

He chuckled. "I had knowledge of her long-running affair with Peter Sanderson, a man a decade her junior. Dear ol' Betsy was completely smitten over him. I managed to get my hands on his stationary and forge his handwriting to pen her a letter announcing that he was coming to her that night."

Lord Devere lunged toward the man with the musket.

As quickly as Devere moved, Wilson was even quicker in whipping out his sword to bar Lord Devere's progress. For an instant, she feared the sword would pierce Lord Devere's body.

But both men showed restraint.

"I will drive this through you," Wilson hissed.

"And when you do," Lord Devere quipped, "Miss Robinson and the priest will be able flee. I'm willing to die to save them— and to see that you're brought to justice."

"No!" she screamed. "Kill me. I'm the one who saw you that night in Devon."

"Don't listen to her," Lord Devere shouted. "She's just saying that to save the rest of us."

A sinister look on his face, Wilson's gaze shifted from her to Lord Devere. Then he took a step toward his lordship, and Lord Devere stepped back. Wilson's gaze never left her. "I want you, Miss Robinson, to move closer to Lord Devere."

Puzzled, she moved next to him.

Wilson then directed his attention to the priest. "You, too, come closer and stand next to the others."

She could not understand what this madman was planning,

but she was terrified he'd drive his sword through Lord Devere.

"Now, Goddard, you're to aim your musket at Miss Robinson. If anyone moves, you're to shoot her."

Wilson then re-sheathed his sword and turned to exit the church. "I shall be right back."

Was he going to get another musket? Dread crept to every cell in her body. She was going to die and, because of her, Lord Devere was, too.

The door burst back open, and Wilson stood there, holding a coiled rope. "Nothing to worry about. I'm just going to tie the three of you together."

She was still perplexed. It wasn't as if a single musket ball could skip from one to the other.

As the man referred to as Goddard pointed the musket at them, Wilson proceeded to bind three pair of trembling hands, then three pair of feet, and last, he strung the three of them together. When he was finished, he stood back and laughed in a most gleeful fashion.

What diabolical plan had his evil mind hatched? She was soon to find out.

"What a pity," Wilson said. "I'm going to set this church on fire, and the three of you will perish in the blaze—if not from smoke inhalation. And that wretched church registry will perish with you."

She knew it would do no good to beg him to spare Lord Devere and the priest.

The young priest's voice shook when he said, "You know you're going to hell."

Wilson laughed even louder. "I believe neither in heaven nor in hell nor in your God." He moved to the altar and spent a few moments starting a fire.

He strode back to the rear of the church. "We'll leave now, Goddard."

Goddard walked backward, aiming the musket at them until he reached the door. When Wilson opened the door, a stream of bright sunlight flooded the church, but only for a moment before the door slammed as they fled.

Her eyes began to water from the smoke that was beginning to rise in the sacristy.

"Caroline," Lord Devere whispered, "there's a knife in my left boot. See if you can wiggle your hand in there and reach it."

In small increments, she managed to turn herself around. Fortunately, her hands—even bound together as they were—were slender enough for her to reach inside his boot and extract the sheathed knife.

Her gaze locked with his as she placed it in his bound hands. He managed to unsheathe the knife. "Let me get yours first."

She rocked on her bottom until she reached the front of him and offered her hands. Seconds later, he'd cut through the rope. She then took the knife and slashed the ropes at his and the priest's hands, then their feet and her own.

"Come," Devere said, "we'll go out the back door. They may be watching the church burn." Knife in hand, he led the way.

She had no doubt the vile Wilson would be gleefully watching the church.

"I must get our register," the priest said in a shaky voice between sputtering coughs.

The church was filling with smoke.

"Is there a back way to get to the tavern where my men are?" Devere asked the priest.

"Yes, I'll show you." The clergyman then collected the oversized book which had recorded births and marriages for hundreds of years.

It distressed her that this old church would be destroyed, but saving human life was more important. By now, flames had caught and climbed to the roof over the sacristy.

"We've got to hurry," Devere said.

From the door at the west side of the back of the church, they followed the priest. Terrified still of being seen, she was pleased that tall, flowering rhododendron provided cover, as long as their group stooped.

Moments later, they reached the tavern. When his lordship's servants saw the look on their employer's face, they sobered. "Is something amiss, my lord?" the coachman asked.

"Yes. Come with me." He turned back to Caroline. "You and the priest stay here until I come for you."

"No! I'm coming with you. I'll not sit here while my church burns to the ground," the priest said.

A look of outrage swept across the tavernkeeper's clean-shaven face. "If our church is on fire, I'm coming, too. We'll not allow our church to burn." He threw off his apron and rushed after the others.

His hand still clutching the knife, Lord Devere hurried from the building with a total of eight men following him.

She wanted to go, too, but after all the trouble she'd wrought, she couldn't bear to go against his lordship's wishes.

HE ORDERED THE coachman and groom to grab their muskets from his coach, which was just in front of the tavern. Then all the men charged toward the burning church. Set a hundred yards away from the church was a fine equipage. It had to be Wilson's.

By now, a dozen more villagers had seen the flames coming from their church and were bearing down on it, some with water buckets, and all of them shouting.

Devere eyed his servants. "Come with me to that coach opposite the church."

As they approached Wilson's carriage, Goddard, sitting next to the armed coachman, saw them and started to draw his weapon.

"If they act as if they're going to shoot, you fire first," Devere told his men.

Just as Goddard's musket came up, Devere's coachman fired.

Goddard clutched at his chest and fell to the ground, crimson staining his soiled clothing.

Seeing that shot, Wilson's coachman threw down his gun and held up his hands.

Wilson yanked open his coach door, and his eyes rounded when he saw Devere bearing down on him. His sword whipped out and he leapt from the carriage, his feet landing four feet from Devere.

Devere regretted he'd not brought his own sword. "You're finished, Wilson."

Even when Devere's groom closed in on them, Wilson was not to be deterred. He lunged toward Devere, but Devere twisted away. Devere stabbed his attacker's arm to disable him, but he missed. His dagger plunged instead into the man's heart.

As Wilson dropped to the ground, it was obvious he had not survived the knife wound. Devere looked down at the man. His face was distorted, and a vast amount of blood pooled on his chest, trailing into a larger pool on the dirt in which he breathed his last breath. Devere felt not a drop of remorse. Rid of such evil, the world was a better place.

IT WAS COMPLETELY dark by the time they managed to quell the fire in the church. Devere vowed to pay for the restoration of the building. Wilson's coachman, who had been ignorant of and outraged by his master's nefarious acts, had agreed to take the two dead bodies back to London. Later, Devere would sort out that business with the city's magistrates.

He engaged rooms at the inn for himself and Caroline and for his coachman and groom to take shelter above the stables. He'd also ordered that his and Miss Rutherford's dinners be served in his private parlor. They hadn't eaten since that magical picnic a dozen hours earlier. Was that the same day? It seemed a year had passed since then.

When she walked through the door to his parlor, he rose to greet her. Then, previously unaware that he was going to do it, he moved to her and drew the cherished woman into his embrace.

She collapsed against him, her arms wrapping him tightly.

Neither spoke for a moment. The horror and terror and, in the end, absolution of the day had drawn them together more powerfully than familial ties.

Finally, he spoke. "Come, Caroline. I think a glass of wine will settle you after today's harrowing events."

They went to the table, and he poured the Madeira. "A toast. To you, Caroline. May you always be a part of the Beresford family."

She said nothing but tapped his glass with hers, and they both drank. They then proceeded to eat their roast beef and potatoes. It was impossible for him to concentrate on his food when his desire for her consumed him like a raging fire. As each bite passed her lips, he longed for those lips. The rise and fall of her chest made him want to see her breasts, to feel them, to taste them.

When her lashes lowered, he found it incredibly seductive. He allowed himself to imagine that provocative look was for him. He permitted himself to imagine the ecstasy of lying with her, bare flesh to bare flesh.

And he thought he could go mad with want.

When the last bite had been cleaned from her plate, he could resist her no more. He moved to her chair where he lowered his head and began to nibble on the satin smoothness of her delicate neck. She made no move to stop him.

"Will you allow me to kiss you again?" he murmured into her ear.

She answered him by standing, facing him, a hunger in her eyes that matched his own. He crushed her to him, cupping her buttocks, pressing her against his now-bulging erection as he nearly devoured her with a passionate kiss.

The way she greedily suckled at his probing tongue and her throaty little moans told him she wanted exactly what he wanted. More than once, he had to stop himself from begging her to come to his bed.

She was, after all, his employee. If he asked, he believed she would comply, but he cared too deeply for her to take advantage of her. He gently eased away. Their eyes locked. To him, she was the most beautiful woman in the world. Because he loved her. He had most thoroughly fallen in love with Caroline, Charlotte, or Miss Rutherford or Miss Robinson, it mattered not. This woman standing before him, her skin reddened from his stubble, had captured his heart.

"I want to be yours," she whispered.

CHAPTER NINETEEN

I T WASN'T JUST this overpowering desire to unite with him that brought on Caroline's decision to give herself to the man she loved. His very touch had always ignited this desire that thrummed through her body. And always, she had resisted that final act they both craved.

How fitting it was that now—now that she knew without a doubt this man loved her—she belonged to him. Completely. It mattered not that he could never offer marriage. He offered so much more.

He'd proven his love. He would have given his life to preserve hers. Few women could ever claim a love that powerful. Nor could they ever find a man who was the equal of Henry Beresford, the Sixth Earl of Devere.

Hers was not to question how someone as plain and penniless as she could have won his affections. Yet, his love was undeniable; hers, unstoppable.

When she'd left him in the adjoining chamber, she had fully intended to undress herself and don her night shift, but she proved incapable of unlacing her stays. The very thought of having Devere remove them sent her pulse skittering.

Barefoot, she padded to the door and eased it open. "It seems I may need some assistance." She held back from adding, *my darling.*

"Your stays?"

Of course, he would know about such things. She nodded shyly.

He came into the candlelit chamber. Gone were his coat and shirt. Even his boots had been removed. He stood there only in his breeches, the candlelight flickering over his bronzed flesh. His magnificence robbed her of breath.

She watched with heavy-lidded eyes as he moved behind her. He dropped a path of butterfly kisses on her neck before he began to unlace her stays. When her breasts sprang free, a liquid heat gushed to her core.

Surprisingly unembarrassed over her nakedness, she turned and flowed into his arms.

They soon moved to the bed. She slid across the fine linen sheets that had come from Devere House, wordlessly encouraging him to lie beside her. She felt a hollow ache, the desire to draw him into her body, to be possessed by him.

He blew out the bedside candle. In the velvety darkness, his breeches fell to the floor, and soon he was lying beside her, drawing her into his arms, loving her to completion. As he clenched over her, both of them nearly undone by overlapping spasms of pleasure, he cried out, "God, but I love you, my Caroline."

Long afterwards, both sated, she lay in the heat of him, his muscled arm pulling her close. Her love for him was more powerful than ever. Even knowing she—an unmarried lady—could be carrying his seed caused not the slightest remorse. Loving him could never bring shame. Every breath she drew was for him. Her love.

HE AWAKENED THE next morning before she did. For a long while, he gazed at her sweet, lightly freckled face and was nearly overcome with a heady sense of possession. This was the woman he yearned to protect. Always. This was the woman he loved.

Eventually, he left the bed and dressed before going downstairs and requesting that their breakfast be brought to his chamber. He then went to the churchyard where plump pink rhododendron bloomed, and he snapped off a handful of them to present to the woman he loved.

Back at the inn, he secured a tall vase for the flowers and set them on the table where they would break their fast in his private parlor. By the time she had awakened and dressed for the day in that mint green dress that had been Harry's, the breakfast offerings stood ready at the table.

When she opened the bedchamber door, it was if his heart rejoiced. "Good morning, my love."

Her eyes danced. "Good morning to you, my dearest."

He knew for certain at that moment that he wanted to see this woman's face across the breakfast table from him every morning of his life. "You look lovely."

"I brought this dress because I knew you admired me in it." Her gaze whisked to the flowers. "Did you pick the rhododendron?"

"I did."

"I love them. Thank you very much." She came to sit at the chair he had scooted out for her, and they proceeded to eat in silence. There was so much he wanted to say, things he'd never before said to any woman. Caroline was not just any woman. Of all the women in the kingdom, it was she, and she alone, who had been created for him. She was his. Forever.

It had been difficult these past several weeks to articulate his feelings. He knew now it was because this profound love was so new an experience that he'd not understood it.

He watched as she gracefully poured tea into their cups and, their food eaten, sat back and regarded him with a bemused expression on her beloved face.

Finally, he stood and began to pace the chamber. "I have a

confession."

A worried look swiped across her face.

"I've neglected to inform you of a most important . . . occurrence," he went on.

Her face blanched. "Pray, do not tell me you have a secret wife."

He shook his head. "No, not that."

"Then . . .?"

"Well, forgive me if I blunder. I have no experience in these matters."

"What matters?" she asked.

"I have been remiss now for quite some time in telling you that I've fallen in love."

Her brows dipped low.

Seeing her distress, he rushed to her. "Oh, but it's you! You're the one who's stolen my heart."

Now she burst into tears.

He fell to his knees beside her chair as he cradled her upper torso into his embrace. "I believe I fell in love with you that first day when I glimpsed you standing on top of that chair, terrified of that mouse. You looked so vulnerable, I wanted to hold you in my arms and love you forever."

Her cries grew more audible.

"Have I offended you?"

She vehemently shook her head.

"Good. While I'm on my knees, I might as well do the deed and beg for your hand in marriage."

She wailed.

"Are you sure I haven't offended you?"

"I'm . . ." Sniff. Sniff. "Sure."

"Allow me to phrase it as you deserve. Will you, my dearest Caroline, become my countess?"

Still weeping, she eagerly nodded.

He retrieved his handkerchief and blotted her tears. "Now we won't have to change your name from Rutherford to Robinson or

Robinson to Rutherford. You'll simply be known as Lady Devere."

"I care not for titles. It's you I care for. I have loved you almost as long as I've resided under your roof."

A laugh spurted from his lips. "It was the same for me. I'd never given much thought before to *fate*, but I now realize you were my fate. I suppose I could even be indebted to that vile Robert Wilson for bringing you to me."

She shook her head. "I refuse to credit that murderer for something so wonderful. Allow me to believe my father is playing matchmaker from heaven. I know he would have greatly admired you."

"You're just saying that because I'm a Whig."

"That's only one of the reasons I love you."

She slid off the chair and into his embrace.

THE FOLLOWING AFTERNOON, instead of going straight to Curzon Street, they went to Cavendish Square to see how Great-aunt Margaret was progressing and to see if Harriett was able to come home with them.

"Our great-aunt is napping," Harriett said. "Perhaps I can run home and check my birds. I should die if I missed the birth of the fledglings."

"So Great-aunt Margaret still needs you?" Devere asked.

"Indeed she does, and I'm happy to help."

"But you miss your pets," Caroline said. She'd come to know Lady Harriett so well.

"Indeed I do."

Caroline nodded sympathetically. "Could you not bring Pumpkin here?"

Lady Harriett's face transformed. "That would answer very well. You are so clever, my dear Miss Rutherford." She linked her arm to Caroline's as they departed the great-aunt's house.

Devere gave a mock cough. "Ah, Harry, it seems that Miss Rutherford is not actually Miss Rutherford."

The coachman opened the carriage door, and they climbed in. "What do you mean?" she asked.

"Her given name was Charlotte Robinson, but she was forced to change her identity. The man who murdered her former employer intended to kill her because he believed she could identify him as the killer."

Harriett yelped. As she yelped, she eyed Caroline, seated across the coach from her, beside her brother. This was highly unusual. Caroline always sat next to her. Harriett's gaze shifted from her brother to Caroline and back again, and recognition sparked in her eyes. "Allow me to guess . . . my brave and courageous brother was able to foil the plot, apprehend the vile killer, and rescue the maiden in distress, the maiden with whom he's fallen in love. How am I doing?"

"You see, your sister is exceedingly clever, my love."

"She is far more mature than I'd credited her."

"So, am I to gain a new sister?" Harriett asked.

"You are," he said.

"Then allow me to say, my dear brother, you are far more mature than I'd credited. You could not have found a more suitable bride—nor one I could ever favor over Miss, er, Caroline. Or do I call you Charlotte?"

Charlotte looked up into the eyes of the man who was to become her husband. "Devere says I will always be Caroline to him, so that is what I shall use."

"I'm so happy. When's the wedding?"

"I get a special license today," he said. "We hope to wed by Friday."

Harriett bit at her lip. "I hope Alex is able to be here for the wedding."

"Why shouldn't he?" Devere asked.

"His father finally died yesterday morning."

"I know he's been ailing for a long while," Devere said. "I shall go to Alex this afternoon."

After a few somber moments, Harriett said, "Oh, Devere, you shall have to take your bride to Hamberly for your wedding trip."

"We couldn't leave you," Caroline protested.

"Fiddle! I shall continue on with Great-aunt Margaret, and hopefully by the time you return to London, her ankle will be healed."

"I think we could leave her, love," he said, peering down at Caroline. "I shall charge Alex with looking after her. Between Great-aunt Margaret and him, Harry won't be able to get into any mischief."

Harriett sent him a mock glare.

Once they arrived at Devere House, they went together to Harriett's study to see if the eggs had hatched. "I keep the door to my study closed at all times to keep my kitties away. I couldn't bear any more murders."

"Nor can we," Devere said, throwing an arm around his betrothed.

"I was speaking of the murder to my beloved pets," Harriett said, glaring at her teasing brother.

When Harriett looked at the cage, she squealed with delight. A pair of tiny birds tilted their heads, opened beaks, toward the mother's offering. Harriett raced to the cage.

Devere and Caroline came to stand behind her. The fledglings' parents, their gender indistinguishable, perched lovingly over them.

Her face aglow, Harriett turned around. "Love birds, just like you two."

EPILOGUE

"WE ARE IN possession of information that proves Mrs. Wilson was not legally wed to Robert Wilson," Devere said to his bride-to-be on the eve of their wedding. "What do you propose we do about it?"

"How much did you tell the magistrates about Wilson's ill deeds?"

"First, I told them that Charlotte Robinson did not kill Betsy Wyndham. I intimated that Robert Wilson may have hired killers to slay his former lover as well as my footman while they attempted to commit a theft at my house on Curzon Street. The magistrates were already acquainted with two thieves named Johnson and Goddard, and they have since linked them to Wilson." He chuckled.

"What do you find so amusing?"

"It just occurred to me my solicitor may be returning to tell me that Charlotte Robinson slayed Mrs. Wyndham. Just one more story I may have to refute."

As he'd spoken to her, she could hear the love in his voice. She didn't know what she had ever done to deserve his love, but she vowed to be the best wife a man could ever have. She did believe life had its compensations. She'd dealt with heavy losses, heartache, and unspeakable danger. Now, this blissful happiness that consumed her compensated for all previous suffering.

"I have learned," she said, "that Mr. and Mrs. Robert Wilson are the parents of five children. Those children, the eldest of whom now have children of their own, have done nothing to merit being tainted as illegitimate. Since we and the Birkenfield priest are the only ones who know of the earlier marriage, I don't believe any good could come of nullifying the later marriage."

Devere smiled at her. "It seems we are once again in agreement, my love." He rose from the library sofa, where they'd been sitting. "And now I will go see Lord Rockingham."

Her brows raised in query.

"That's Alex's title now that his father is gone."

IT WAS FITTING that the new Lord Rockingham, his best friend in all the world, stood next to Devere at the front of the church on his wedding day. With the exception of his sisters, Sophia and Mary, who were hundreds of miles away, all the people who mattered to him were here today. His gaze fanned from Harriett to Great-aunt Margaret and came to rest on Caroline as she glided down the nave toward him.

Her dress of simple ivory had no adornment, save for a lacy nosegay of white roses affixed to her long white gloves. No adornment was needed. She was sheer perfection.

His worries that she'd be nervous proved unfounded. A radiant smile on her face, her eyes never left his as she came to take her place beside him. Their hands clasped as they faced the vicar.

When the vicar said matrimony was ordained for the procreation of children, a blossoming sense of well-being unfurled inside of him. The Beresfords who had gone before him would be happy to see this day.

An overwhelming rush of affection seized him when the woman he loved spoke these words: "I, Charlotte/Caroline, take thee, Henry, to my wedded husband, to have and to hold from this day forward, for better, for worse, for richer, for poorer, in sickness and in health, to love, cherish, and to obey, till death us do part, according to God's holy ordinance; and thereto I give thee my troth."

He had waited two-and-thirty years to find his perfect mate, and he'd found her in his Caroline. Today, they would travel to Hamberly, where Beresfords had resided for more than three hundred years. Tonight, she would lie in his arms, the Sixth Countess of Devere, and, hopefully, the mother of the Seventh Earl of Devere. This was unquestionably the happiest day of his life.

As they left the church, she looked up at him. "You truly meant it when you told me that first day, I'd be one of your family."

He smiled down at her. "Henceforth, it's *our* family, my love."

About the Author

Since her first book was published to acclaim in 1998, Cheryl Bolen has written more than three dozen Regency-set historical romances. Several of her books have won Best Historical awards, and she's a *New York Times* and *USA Today* bestseller as well as an Amazon All Star whose books have been translated into nine languages. She's also been penning articles about Regency England and giving workshops on the era for more than twenty years.

In previous lives, she was a journalist and an English teacher. She's married to a recently retired college professor, and they're the parents of two grown sons, both of whom she says are brilliant and handsome! All four Bolens (and their new daughter-in-law) love to travel to England, and Cheryl loves college football and basketball and adores reading letters and diaries penned by long-dead Englishwomen.

Check out these sites of hers:
subscribe to newsletter – littl.ink/newsletter
blog – blogl.ink/RegencyRamblings
website – www.CherylBolen.com
facebook – fbl.ink/Facebook
Pinterest – littl.ink/Pinterest
Readers' group – facebook.com/groups/2586590498319473

CPSIA information can be obtained
at www.ICGtesting.com
Printed in the USA
LVHW061304030122
707736LV00021B/276